catching
RAVEN

lauren michelle

Chasing Mia (originally published as *Take Heart*) is Lauren Michelle's debut novel

—Too good to put down!—
"I read this book in one sitting! Very addicting. I laughed, I cried. Definitely worth a read. Can't wait for more!"

—Tori Smith

—Ready for book 2—
"It's hard to believe this is Lauren's first novel considering her writing style. I was quickly connected to the characters and enjoyed every page!"

—H. Brown

—Great read—
"It could almost be one of the best books I've read this year. I cried a few times. My heart hurt for Mia and Chase, but I also laughed during other parts! Would love to read more from these characters. Would love to read more from Eric and Raven."

—L. Wimer

catching RAVEN

PROLOGUE

e r i c

Four Years Ago....

I swear I've been here a thousand times before.

Well, not exactly. I've only lived in Austin for a couple weeks now. But generally speaking, self-destruction is a process I'm all too familiar with. It's second nature. And that's exactly what I'm doing when I bring Nina back to my uncle's place. I'm not looking for companionship. I'm just looking for a distraction. She's the third one this week. If it weren't for Max working nights, I'd never be able to get away with servicing this much pussy.

Nina knows anything beyond sex isn't up for discussion. I made that abundantly clear when she approached me last weekend at Levi's party. Since she's fresh off a breakup, she's not looking for anything more than a quick, meaningless rebound. Talk about a win-win.

"Your parents aren't home, are they?" she asks.

"Nope."

"Then you should take me to your room."

"Already on the agenda."

Her eager fingers work at my belt in between kisses. I slip her the tongue and start walking us backwards. She kicks her shoes off at the bottom of the stairs. Halfway up, my shirt is next to go. We stumble down the hall, colliding with numerous walls, and barge into my bedroom. Bedsprings squeak in protest when we collapse on the mattress. Impatient, I tug her shirt up and over her head, then kiss her hard once more and pull away to stand up.

"Take your shorts off."

Much to my appreciation, she does. And she makes a seductive show out of it. I strip down to my boxers and grab a condom from my dresser, then walk back over to the bed and slide her underwear down her luscious thighs, admiring the view along the way. When they're off, she unabashedly lets her legs fall open, granting me full access.

Sex with no obligations. Is there anything better?

"It's a great day to be me."

"Yes, it is, Eric."

I grin at her lack of modesty and rip the foil packet open. Once I'm ready, I crawl over her and spread her thighs even wider apart, moving in on the target.

"Holy hell!" she gasps as I enter her.

She runs her fingers through my hair and grabs two fistfuls. I love how shameless she is. So hot and refreshing. Her hips grind against the pressure. I reward her by reaching down and focusing on her clit. She releases my hair and starts playing with her nipples. The erotic view spurs me on even more.

"Ah, just like that. Don't stop," she instructs.

I don't. We go at it until we both feel equally raw and thoroughly used. I kick up the pace, itching to receive the ultimate sedation. Anything to shut my brain off. I thrust hard and fast until she shudders and cries out my name. Stuck in my own fantasy, I make a catastrophic error. "Oh, God, Rave," I say, upon reaching climax.

Nina freezes.

Everything stops, minus my body still trembling uncontrollably inside hers. Even though the lights are off, I can feel her intense gaze boring into mine, stripping me bare.

"What did you just call me?"

I groan and run a free hand through my hair, exhaling my discomfort. What the hell do I say to her? Hate feeling exposed. *What the fuck, Eric?* "Nina, I'm so sorry. It was a slip up."

She pushes me off and stands up, shielding her body protectively. "Don't ever call me again you piece of shit."

I wince. Before I can apologize further or find some lame way to explain, she's gone.

How's that for a night of self-destruction?

I punch my headboard and roll off the bed, then remove the condom and get dressed. No idea what to do next. All I know is I desperately need another distraction. One to offset tonight's disaster. One to make me feel a whole lot less shitty about myself than I do right now.

Levi and I are busy marking up an old cement wall when a couple of voices in the distance interrupt our creative flow. We stop spraying and listen, trying to decipher if the unexpected company is a threat or not. A twig snaps, followed by crunching debris. My heart starts pounding. Beads of sweat trickle down the sides of my temple. I attempt to swallow, but my throat is too dry. Aerosol and paranoia swirl in the air; an unwelcome reminder of home. My gut's already telling me what I need to know. These aren't random passersby.

Breathe in; breathe out.

Another twig snaps.

They're trying to be sneaky but failing miserably.

I squeeze the spray can as hard as I can until my fingers ache. Anything to help dispel the rising panic. *Must concentrate.* I smother the flashlight against my hoodie and lean forward to listen for the faintest of noises, trying to gauge how close they are. It always comes down to this. The thrill. The chase.

Us versus them.

Levi peers around the corner of the cement wall and attempts to spot them from above. His jet-black hair shields him from detection—a stark contrast from my pale blond. Blending in with the night is crucial during times like these. It can mean all the difference between getting caught and escaping. To our advantage, we've been doing this for years. We know the drill. Flipside, there are one too many streetlights for my comfort.

Levi ducks back down under the overpass and points upward, indicating that the cops are on his side of the bridge. I nod and reach down to grab my backpack. I slip the paint and flashlight inside, then zip it closed and sling it over my shoulder, extra mindful not to make a sound. The two of us backtrack and crawl up the opposite side, away from the voices.

Once we're out of view, we rest our backs against one of the pillars, bracing ourselves. A few moments later, we hear them approaching. I glance down below at the spot where we were just standing and notice a solid beam of light traveling along the gravel. We'll have to wait until they're completely under the bridge before we make a run for it. Otherwise, we don't stand a chance.

Hushed voices capture my attention. I lean over, straining to hear. One pig tells the other one that we're close by. The graffiti is still fresh and the fumes are potent.

Suddenly, their conversation comes to a halt.

The panic inside me flares, thinking they've found something. I glance over at Levi and his features remain impassive—a strong testament that he's the one who does better under pressure.

My mind scrambles to think of an exit strategy.

Maybe it's less risky if we stay put?

Negative. They'll scan the entire area. They'd be stupid not to.

Taking the lead, Levi crab walks up the hill. I follow suit. Once we reach the pavement, we'll be able to make a break for it. Levi's car is only a block away. I just hope we can make it there without getting caught. It'd be nice to have my record remain jail-free.

We're almost in the clear when my left foot slips against the gravel, sending loose chunks of rock and dirt cascading down the hill. Two flashlights instantly zone in on it, getting brighter and brighter.

Levi and I wrestle to our feet and take off running.

"Hold it! Stay right where you are!" one of them shouts.

We ignore them and bolt toward the car. Adrenaline races through my veins as my feet pound the pavement. I've never run so fast in my life. The officers continue barking orders, but all I can hear is my heartbeat hammering in my ears.

"Go, go, go!" I yell to Levi.

We make it to the car and jump inside. One of the officers breaks off and runs across the street to his squad car. Levi's Grand Am roars to life. He slams his foot on the gas and the car lurches forward, forcing my back against the seat. We speed off toward the interstate. I yank the seatbelt across my chest and strap myself in.

Levi nervously glances in the rearview mirror. Lights and sirens alert the sleeping neighborhood.

"He's gaining on us," I tell him.

"It's two in the morning. There's nobody else on the road to throw him off our trail. We're screwed."

"Not necessarily. Hop on Mopac."

Without missing a beat, he swerves onto a side street, taking a shortcut. The cop mimics our every move, hell bent on catching us. I don't even know where his partner went, but I know it won't be long before others show up.

"Damn it!" Levi smashes his fist against the dash. "I told you downtown was too risky to tag."

I brace myself against the seat and keep my eyes trained on the side mirror. "Calm down, man. Now's not the time to be losing your shit. We have bigger problems to deal with."

"You don't say?" he snaps, making a sudden hard left.

"Aye, how many times have you thrown us into a fucked-up situation and I've had to be the one to bail us out? Return the favor."

His fingers grip the steering wheel. He clenches his jaw and accelerates onto the onramp.

"We have to try to lose him at an exit. Wait until the last possible second before you swerve off. Let's hope his backup doesn't show up before then."

"Doesn't matter anyway. He's probably already run my plates."

It's my turn to glare at him. "We're not going down without a fight. You hear me? It's too late to surrender."

He speeds up, the car matching the frantic rhythm of my heart. Deep down, I know we're screwed. I knew from the moment we heard them on the bridge. We've dodged the cops before, but this time it's different. We didn't think far enough ahead or allow room for error. We started getting too comfortable in the routine—a rookie mistake.

"Grab onto something," Levi orders.

I grip the seat belt strap across my chest and suck in a deep breath. Before I can exhale, Levi swerves to the right to catch a last-minute exit. He overestimates the amount of force needed and the entire car shifts sideways.

A blur of events sweeps by. The cop behind us slams on his brakes and swerves to the left to avoid hitting us. Four sets of tires screech against the pavement, rivaling the pitch of the sirens. Levi and I both shout profanities as the back end of our vehicle crashes into the concrete barrier. Shards of glass explode in the backseat. My head is propelled directly into the passenger window, the impact making me see bright, vivid, translucent colors.

In the blink of an eye, it's all over.

My ears are ringing. I'm fighting to stay conscious. I shift around in my seat, my muscles aching in protest. My head rolls to the side, assessing Levi's condition. His face is buried in a bloodstained airbag. Panic seizes my chest. Mine didn't deploy. Why didn't mine deploy?

With shaky hands, I feel around for the seat belt buckle and release the strap. I lean over the console, spots blurring my vision, and grab onto Levi's shoulder.

I give him a gentle shake. "Levi, wake up."

No response.

I place two fingers below his jaw on his neck. *Thank God, there's a pulse.* Relief floods my chest, but that feeling dissipates the instant the cop opens my door. He ushers me out of the car. I stumble around as if I've been drinking, my weight counter-balanced by his grip. Off in the distance, I hear more sirens.

The officer helps Levi out of the car and makes us both sit down as he proceeds to take stock of our injuries and search our belongings. My head is fucking killing me. I press my sleeve to the side of my temple—the hoodie is blood soaked. Everything's so bright. Why is everything so bright at night?

An ambulance arrives shortly after, along with backup and a tow truck. Normally, I'd refuse to go to the hospital, but given the current situation, ditching Levi is out of the question. Why can't I seem to stop fucking up lately?

As we leave the scene, a wave of guilt washes over me. And all these colors are still coating my vision. Scarlet being the most prominent one.

ONE

e r i c

Hours before the accident...*and the other accident.*

Every other week I'm required to see a therapist. It was one of the conditions my uncle placed on me before he took me in as a kid. Dr. Vivienne Mitchell has been my therapist for the last year. Thank God she's willing to make house calls. She's different from all the other shrinks I've had because she has the decency to talk to me like I'm her client, not her patient. That's key. There's nothing worse than being talked to like you're a sick person when you're not. Doesn't hurt that she's smoking hot, either.

Vivienne opens the file resting on her lap and jots down some notes. Sometimes I wonder if she's just doodling. How hilarious would that be? I'm sitting here spilling my guts and she's drawing cartoons like she's Walt Fucking Disney. Then again, if I had to listen to everyone's problems on a daily basis, I'd probably be sketching too. I'm already antsy to get out of here and we're only fifteen minutes in.

"How are you adjusting to a new school?"

I shrug. "Fine, I guess."

Truth be told, I absolutely hate it here. Transferring right before your senior year blows. It's not like I had any say in the matter. Austin is nothing more than a cheap imitation of a life I used to know. Different house, different people, same predictable bullshit.

"Tell me about your classes. Are you taking anything you like?"

"Art."

She glances up and smiles. Vivienne knows art has always been a huge part of my life. It's my coping mechanism for everything. When I'm sketching or painting, nothing else can interfere. In a house where I constantly had to be on guard, art allowed me to express myself without consequence. It gave me an escape from the never-ending shitstorms and monumental disappointments.

"Are you thinking about joining any extracurricular activities?"

"I've thought about trying out for the track team, but that's not until spring."

"Okay, what about activities outside of school? Any that interest you?"

I know what she's getting at. She wants me to stay out of trouble this year.

"None that you would approve of."

She tilts her frames down and pins me with her gaze.

"You're eighteen now, Eric. You won't be able to get off scot-free anymore. The underage drinking, the graffiti, the fighting—those things will go on an adult record if you get caught."

"I already told you that fight wasn't my fault," I say defensively.

"I understand, but let me ask you a question. Do you honestly believe that Levi had no influence over you that night?"

This is a big bone of contention with us. She doesn't approve of the people I surround myself with, and I'm over her telling me how I should live my life. She thinks some of my friends are bad influences—Levi being the worst. She's not entirely wrong, but I refuse to admit that out loud.

"I make my own decisions."

"Of course you do, but is it possible you would've handled the situation differently had he not been there?"

"If Levi wouldn't have been there, the fight never would've happened in the first place."

"Exactly my point," she says, settling back into the chair. "He's an instigator. That concerns me."

There she goes pretending to be my mother again. Growing frustrated, I run my hands through my hair and lean forward, needing her to understand where I'm coming from.

"Look, he's a good friend who's been there through some dark shit. That's not easy to find. Most people would flake. I'm not saying he's perfect, but he has my back and vice versa. I refuse to cut him off just because you don't approve."

"I'm not telling you to cut him off. I'm simply suggesting that you take a step back and distance yourself for a little while. It might help give you a better perspective."

"A better perspective on what?"

She folds her hands in her lap. "You say he has your back—and perhaps that's true—but you've also told me he has a habit of letting you take the fall for his mistakes. Do you think that's fair?"

"Life isn't fair."

"Eric, you can choose whether or not you want to keep putting yourself in these situations."

"It's not that simple."

"Why not?"

"Next subject."

She picks up her pen and makes a small note. This is how we operate. If she tries to take me somewhere I'm not willing to go, she'll drop it and come back to it later. I know it's just a matter of time before Vivienne makes me revisit my childhood. We've slowly been building up to it. As we get closer and closer, I feel myself detaching and giving fewer and fewer fucks. She'd tell you that's because I'm a *slap a Band-Aid on it and call it good* kinda guy and she's a *we're going to heal this wound properly from the inside out* kinda woman.

Her method is far worse.

"Fill me in on what else is going on," she encourages.

"I applied for another lawn care job."

"Have you heard anything back?"

"Not yet."

"Are you still saving up for a car?"

"Duh. I'm the only eighteen-year-old I know without a car."

"What kind of car are you leaning towards?"

Any hope she had of steering me off this topic went right out the window the second she asked me that question. We spend the rest of the session discussing cars, street racing, and graffiti. I divulge where my favorite spots are to paint, and the areas I'm planning on hitting up tonight after dark. She tries to talk me out of it like the sensible therapist she is, but a hint of a smile manages to escape, betraying her warning. It's nice to be reminded that once in a while, she's actually capable of being cool.

TWO

r a v e n

Present Day

I'm in love with a boy. Not just any boy, a boundary-testing, pussy-chasing scoundrel, who also happens to be one of my best friends. Eric Hansen has been corrupting my world since high school. He was a too-cool-for-school senior—a rebel with many causes—and I was your average overeager freshman, secretly vying for his attention.

I couldn't tell you exactly when the shift happened—when we stopped being ourselves and started being *us*. It was gradual. A slow burn that smoldered over a series of uneventful days, weeks, months, or even years. It snuck up on us, as defining moments often do in one's life. Then it consumed us from the inside out.

Beautiful chaos.

Unfortunately, there are a million and one obstacles standing in the way. The first one is my current beau, Brandon. We met at Bellotti's while I was working one night. He came in to eat dinner with some friends and ended up asking for my number. I admired his confidence, so I said yes. We've been dating for a couple months. He makes me feel good. Cherished.

This brings me to the next obstacle: Eric's perfected the art of getting laid. The endless string of women has become as routine as grabbing a morning coffee. Every time I turn around, there's a new girl in his arms—or in his bed. He loves to treat them to a latte and fry them up some breakfast the next morning. Why not make them feel at home right before you kick them out, right? Eric logic? If there is such a thing. Guess it makes the Walk of Shame more bearable.

I don't want to fall into that same trap and wind up being just another latte girl. It's the biggest reason why I haven't succumbed to his numerous advances throughout the years. Somewhere along the way, he stopped pursuing, and we both found ourselves trapped in the friend zone. Timing is everything, and we suck at it.

"Um, hello? Earth to Raven."

My gaze immediately snaps to my best friend, Tori Reynolds. Anyone in need of a loyal girlfriend who's drama-free? Too bad, suckas—she's all mine. Like twins separated at birth, we clicked and fused six years back. We were two lone chicks swirling in a sea of insecurities, dancing to a Madonna song straight outta the Guy Ritchie era. Insta-love was in motion.

I grab my straw and poke at the ice, then swirl it around and bend forward to take a sip of my lemonade. Leaning back against the booth, I give her my full attention.

"Sorry, my head was off somewhere else. What's up?"

She grabs the pitcher and pours herself another frozen margarita. Doesn't matter that it's the middle of the day and she's underage. Tori neither operates on "suit and tie time," nor does she partake in blatant forms of age discrimination. It's not an easy fight but someone's got to step up and be a shining example in this morally corrupt society of ours. Honestly, what are people thinking these days?

"I was just saying that your birthday is coming up in a couple weeks and we need to plan something spectacular. Is Mia coming back for the summer?"

"Yeah. Her dad's picking her up from the airport next week."

Amelia Foster is another member of the crew. She lives in Kansas most of the year under the oppressive constraints of Mommy Dearest—a woman who is nothing more than an empty vessel for vodka to take human form in. No wonder she stays with her dad during the summer. Glass half-full version: she gets a three-month reprieve. That's something, I guess.

"Aces. I'll shoot her a text tonight and see if she wants to get in on the event planning."

"Don't bother. Mia despises over-the-top décor. Says people place too much emphasis on showing off and not nearly enough thought on the actual experience."

"I'm sure she'd be willing to make an exception for her best friend," Tori argues.

"Grudgingly. And we'd never hear the end of it."

"What if we get her drunk and slip her some penis?"

"Got one stashed away that we can borrow?"

"Maybe," she plays coy. "Speaking of penises, how goes the Eric and Ravenna saga?"

"Same old. Empty promises, messy emotions, insomnia, blue balls, you name it...it happens to us."

"Common side effects of Friend Zone."

"It's the worst."

"Do you ever wonder if Brandon's pretending to be unobservant so that way you'll be more prone to slipping up, giving him the perfect opportunity to catch you in some compromising situation that looks sketchier than it really is? Then, when you least expect it, he'll screw you over?"

"All the time," I respond. "But Brandon doesn't work that way. He's sweet and trusting. Besides, there's nothing to hide. Harmless flirting does not a scandal make."

"And wishful thinking does not a reality become."

"What's that supposed to mean?"

"It means you can sit there and tell yourself that flirting with Eric isn't harmful, but we both know it's just a matter of time before lines get blurred and feelings get crushed."

"Nothing's going to happen. Definitely not while Brandon's in the picture."

"Do you actually believe that?"

Something fiercely protective festers inside me. "It's easy for you to sit there and make assumptions, but you have no idea how our dynamic works. No one does."

"Oh, please. I've had a front-row seat for years. Sorta an expert at this point. Plus, you even said yourself that it's getting harder to ignore your feelings for him."

"Which is true," I admit. "But I've got it under control."

"If you say so," she says, her tone filled with doubt. She glances down to check the time on her phone. Her eyes pop out of her head. "Ooh, I have to cut this short or I'm going to be late." Tori slides out of the booth, stands up, and slings her purse over her shoulder. "Sorry to bail on you like this. I totally lost track of time."

"Where are you going?"

"I have an appointment to get my rainforest waxed."

I grimace. "Lovely."

"I'll keep you posted."

"Please don't."

"Prepare to say goodbye to Cousin Itt. I know you'll miss her dearly."

"Filthy lies."

"Brutal truths."

"Get out of here and call me later."

"No promises. I have a dinner date—hence the Brazilian."

"Now *that* you can keep me updated on."

"I fully intend to. Peace out, Girl Scout."

She bids me farewell with a wave and disappears.

I finish off my plate and cue the waitress, then glance down to check my phone for any missed messages. A text pops up on the screen from my Modern Day James Dean—a.k.a. Eric.

MDJD: *You down for a late-night painting sesh tonight? I'll spring for Rudy's BBQ if you promise to be nice.*

Me: *I could be persuaded with brisket and potato salad. And when am I ever not nice?*

MDJD: *Gee, idk. Maybe when you decided to punch me in the balls last week?*

Me: *That was an accident and you know it!*

MDJD: *Semantics. Anyway, 8. Be there or be square.*

Me: *Word on the street is it's hip to be a square.*

MDJD: *Anyone who uses that phrase is clearly a square.*

Me: *Careful. My fingers are flexing for a ball busting.*

MDJD: *You're a lousy flirt.*

Me: *Says the guy who lives for it.*

I shake my head and smile, then drop the phone inside my bag.

Four Years Ago....

I fall backward onto my bed and stare up at the ceiling. My parents would ground me for an eternity if they knew I was considering sneaking out. My clock says 11:27 p.m. I've been obsessively watching this thing tick by for the last twenty minutes.

Longest twenty minutes of my life.

I grab my sandals, tiptoe out into the hall, and check to make sure everyone's asleep before journeying downstairs. This is the only instance where the sound of my dad's snoring is reassuring, not obnoxious.

Flashes of lightning ripple across the sky, helping me see. As if this wasn't going to be difficult enough, now I have to worry about the threat of thunder shaking the whole house. The faintest noises have me on edge. I've surpassed bold and sneaky and gone straight to reckless and stupid.

When my bare foot hits the bottom step, I slide my shoes on and lightly pad across the tile. I take a deep breath for some extra courage and slip out the back door, leaving a small sliver of my good girl persona behind.

It's hard-to-catch-your-breath humid out. Beads of warm rain gently fall on my exposed skin, making me shiver with anticipation. Soon it will be pouring. Before I can talk myself out of this, I run. I've never been a huge risk-taker, but the freedom of breaking rules feels exhilarating.

My legs pick up speed, eager to reach his place. I can see his glowing porch light ahead. A large canopy hangs from above, shielding the deck. I count the houses as I race by, being careful not to trip and fall. My muscles ache in protest as I round on his house. I jog up the steps and attempt to catch my breath.

There's a light on inside, but no sign of Eric. I'm afraid to knock on the door and wake anyone up. Has he changed his mind? Did plans fall through because of the rain and I didn't get the memo? I hope that's not the case. How embarrassing would that be? This is getting weird. I should go.

Suddenly, a moving shadow is cast on the wall. Eric appears at the window, scaring the crap out of me. He smiles and motions for me to come in. I stay put. Maybe this isn't such a good idea. I don't know him that well. Going inside his house during the middle of the night was never part of the plan. He promised we'd stay in the neighborhood since I was scared of getting caught.

He moves to open the door. "Get inside."

"This wasn't part of the deal," I say breathlessly, still recovering from the run.

"Plans change."

That's it?

"I'm going to need more than that."

He props his forearm up against the doorframe. His shirt rides up an inch or two, exposing a small patch of skin.

"What I have in mind can't be done outside when it's raining."

"What exactly do you have in mind?"

"Come see for yourself."

I look in the direction of my house.

He drops his arm and straightens his posture. "Didn't I say you'd be safe? Nothing's going to happen. If you've changed your mind and don't want to be here, I'll grab a hoodie and walk you back home. Just say the word."

Do I want to leave? No. But I shouldn't be here. This isn't me. I'm not the girl who sneaks out of her house at night, ditching her common sense for a guy. Just once I'd like to be that girl, though.

I step inside and remove my shoes.

"Are we the only ones here?"

"Yeah. My uncle left for work a half hour ago. He won't be back until morning."

"Does he always work nights?"

"Every day but Sunday."

He heads for the kitchen and picks up a dishtowel, then throws it my way. I catch it and pat myself dry, tossing it back when I'm done.

"Thanks."

"Don't mention it."

The house is clean and organized, but I wouldn't use cozy as a word to describe it. The walls are completely bare, minus a wooden sailboat hanging underneath a plaque that reads: *Captain's Quarters*. A navy couch is sitting in the living room next to a swamp green recliner. What really ties everything together is the horrendous shag rug being used as the centerpiece. The style freak inside me is dying a slow, painful death. No excuse. You can live on a tight budget and still be trendy. I've seen it happen.

Eric leads me upstairs. With each room we pass, I try to sneak a peek inside. We come to the end of the hallway, and he opens what I assume is his bedroom door and flips the light on.

That's when my entire perception of Eric unravels.

Rich, vibrant brush strokes caress my senses, luring me in. "Oh, my God," I whisper, taking five small steps into the room and spinning around. Explosions of color breathe life into the small space. My jaw drops as I attempt to take everything in. It's too much. All the beauty, creativity, art; it hits you all at once. This couldn't be more of a contrast from the rest of the house. I'm not only impressed; I'm envious. He needs to come over and decorate my room. Like, yesterday.

I turn around to face him. He's leaning against his dresser, watching me. "Did you do all these?" I motion around the room. I can't shake the pure wonder and fascination in my voice.

"Most of them. A few are from other artists. Do you like them?"

I look at him like he's crazy. "*Like* them? Eric, these are amazing. Where did you learn to do this?" I ask, studying the pieces more closely.

"When I was seven, my mom signed us up for an art class. We'd spend a couple hours a week drawing and painting together, trying to imagine how our lives could be. It was our escape. She was always running from something, and I was always looking for a distraction, so it clicked. It's stuck with me ever since."

I don't know what to say. His raw honesty is unexpected. He's usually closed off and guarded. Not wanting to let this rare opportunity pass me by, I blurt, "Can I ask you something?"

"Go for it."

"What happened to your parents? I've heard the rumors, but I don't believe—"

"What rumors?"

My mouth snaps shut. *Crap.* We stare at each other, unsure of what to do next. This is none of my business. I shouldn't even be asking.

"Tell me," he coaxes, sensing my anxiety.

He deserves to know. If it were me, I'd want to know what was being said behind my back. "I heard you were taken away from your parents because they were drug addicts." Definitely didn't come out as smooth as I wanted. Mentally facepalming myself.

He grips the edge of the dresser, his body taut and rigid. "Not exactly. What else have you heard?"

When I don't offer anything more, he waits patiently. My shoulders slump. "I also heard you were expelled from your last school for beating someone up."

"That's definitely not true," he refutes. "I've never been expelled."

"Then why do you have a bruise on your cheek and stitches in the side of your head? That wasn't from a fight?"

"No," he says, averting his gaze and shifting around uncomfortably.

Before I can ask him to elaborate, he cuts the conversation short and strides across the room to crack open a window. He comes to stand directly in front of me, hovering. "Tell you what, let me go get all the supplies we need and we can continue this conversation while we paint. Anything I tell you has to stay between us, though."

If it were possible, this night just got better.

"Absolutely."

"And you have to be willing to share some stuff too," he bargains. "Otherwise, the deal's off."

I nod, more than willing to make that trade.

He bends over to pull a tarp out from under his bed. I move out of the way and crouch down to help. We cover as much of the floor as possible.

"I'll be right back."

He stands up and exits the room. I'm left in silence, listening to the pitter-patter of rain outside. It's calming and serene. I'm not worried about getting caught anymore. I'm not worried about Eric turning out to be a psychopath, rapist, serial killer, or worse—totally lame. No matter what happens when I get home, tonight's already been worth the risk.

THREE

eric

"Why did you move here?" she inquires.

We're sitting cross-legged on the tarp, an array of colors and brushes spread out before of us. My favorite Incubus CD is playing in the background. We each have our own canvas. I offered to let her use the easel, but she declined. I didn't want her sitting alone on the floor, so I volunteered to sit next to her, babysit her project. It's a real inconvenience, let me tell you. My eyes won't stay put. They keep drifting over to her face every so often. Beauty is inspiring, but Raven's is distracting.

"My uncle changed locations for his job. They were understaffed and having trouble finding someone who was willing to work nights at the factory, so they offered to up his salary and relocate him. He took the position without even telling me ahead of time."

"Are you mad?"

"So pissed. Everything I've always known is in Dripping Springs. We didn't just move houses; we uprooted our entire lives. All my friends live there. And I'm farther away from my mom now, too. I know it's only a thirty-minute drive, but that's almost worse. Can you imagine being so close to everything and everyone you know, but have no real way of getting there? It blows. That's why I've been saving up for a car."

"Where does your mom live?" she asks, dipping her brush into midnight and stroking the canvas. Little does she know, that's my favorite color.

"Depends on the month. She bounces around from place to place. Last I heard, she was staying with a friend in Wimberley. I try to go see her when I can, but she can't seem to stay in one place for more than a month or two. She's always had trouble getting her shit together. It's one of the reasons why she gave up custody. She was only sixteen when she had me, and she was forced to sacrifice a lot. Eventually, it all caught up with her. She resents me for that, along with a variety of other reasons. She's not a drug addict, though. No clue where that rumor came from."

Her grip loosens on the paintbrush.

"Careful," I catch the end and slide it back into her palm. "These are oil-based paints. They'll stain your clothes."

"I won't miss this outfit."

"I will," I mutter without thinking. *Shit.* What the hell am I doing? She's only fourteen. I may be impulsive, but I'm not stupid. She's got jailbait written all over her. I rack my brain for a subject change. "What about your parents?"

"They own Bellotti's."

"The restaurant downtown?"

"Yep."

Why didn't I make that connection? It's her last name, dumbass.

"So I'm assuming you're related to Andre, then?"

"Absolutely not," she deadpans, then adds, "He's one of my older brothers."

"That's what I thought. He's a big deal at school. I've only been here a couple weeks and already I've seen countless people kissing his ass. No offense."

"None taken. Story of my life. I'm much closer to Emilio. I could take or leave Andre," she jokes.

"Is Emilio your brother too?"

She nods.

"How many siblings do you have?"

"Three. Two older brothers and a younger sister. Andrea and Arianna are the favorites. When your oldest brother is the beloved quarterback of the high school football team and your little sister is the child who can do no wrong, it's easy to feel outshined. That's why Emilio and I stick together."

"Makes sense. I'm glad I'm an only child. Never had to deal with any sibling rivalry."

"Not to mention Middle Child Syndrome," she adds.

"That too."

I don't know what I'm getting myself into, but so far, Raven's presence makes life seem less shitty. She may be younger, but I think Vivienne would approve. Or maybe she wouldn't because of the age difference. Either way, who really cares? Raven and I are just friends.

For the next two hours, we paint. She decides to call it a night around two in the morning. I walk her back home in the pouring rain and watch her slip inside with a huge smile on her face. I did that. I'm also the first person she's ever snuck out with. This whole night has me grinning like an idiot. Makes the probation I'm on seem less restricting. See? I don't have to give up all my fun.

I wander back to my uncle's house and spend the better part of the night staring at the ceiling. I let my thoughts run wild, entertaining dangerous possibilities I know I'll never have.

Present Day
Sam's Ceramics

A bell jingles, followed by the sound of the front door opening and closing. I carefully set the clay figurines down on the table and lean back to peer around the corner. Raven slips her shoes off and lifts her chin to greet me with a bright smile, her long dark hair spilling around her shoulders.

"Hey you. Some leftover Rudy's is on the kitchen counter. It's still hot, so help yourself."

"Don't mind if I do," she says.

She scurries into the kitchen and grabs a plate from one of the cupboards above her head. Stealing a fork, she piles on the food and embellishes it with a ribbon of BBQ sauce, then sets the bottle down and licks her fingers.

"God, I haven't had Rudy's in forever."

"Me neither. Purchased some figurines while I was here. Thought we'd switch it up and paint some of those tonight."

"What are my choices?" she asks, biting off a piece of brisket.

I glance down at the display in front of me.

"We have a coffee mug, an outline of Texas, a flower vase, and a jar."

"I'll take the coffee mug."

"Never saw that coming," I say, my tone dripping with sarcasm. My fingers wrap around the handle and move the mug to her side of the table. I reserve the jar for me.

"Was Sam working today?"

"Isn't he always?"

"Did y'all get a chance to talk before he left?"

"Sure did. He says 'hi' by the way. He misses you."

Sam is the store owner. He knows us both by name and lets us hang out here whenever we want. He should, seeing as how I single-handedly keep him in business. Every spare dollar I earn goes to supporting his shop. The guy's been my art supplier for years.

Raven tilts her head to the side and smiles warmly. My chest tightens. She's always so pretty when she's relaxed. Less and less of that beauty surfaces these days. I don't even think she realizes it. If I were dating What's His Face, I'd be unhappy too.

Why does she insist on hanging on to him? That guy's a joke. I abruptly break eye contact and focus on organizing the paint colors, fighting to keep my emotions concealed.

"How's Brandon?" A question I feel obligated to ask, but one I don't actually care to know the answer to.

"He's fine," she replies curtly.

Confirms what I already knew. They're still together. A familiar pang of disappointment shoots through me. "What do you see in him?"

She pauses, then slowly sets her plate down on the counter and wipes her mouth with a paper towel. "Well, for starters, he has no problem admitting how he really feels about me."

Does she seriously have the nerve to say that to my face? Unreal. Of all the arguments she could have made, she chose the weakest one.

"Yeah, if only there was a decent guy who was really into you over the last year..."

"That doesn't count. You were only in it for the chase."

"The hell I was. You wanted safe and stable, so you chose Brandon. And now you're torn because you got way more than you bargained for. You can't have it both ways. Either you take the risk with me or go with boring."

"Wow. Jealous much?"

"What's there to be jealous of?"

She narrows her gaze. "You tell me."

He's sharing a bed with my girl. He gets to touch her in places I fantasize about. He gets to hear her deepest desires. She shouts his fucking name, not mine.

"Can't think of anything off the top of my head," I lie.

"Good. Glad we got that settled. Wouldn't want you to catch feelings or anything. Can you imagine the horror? Being forced to open up to another human being and connect? My God. No wonder you're not ready for commitment."

What a sassy little b— "Who are you to tell me what I'm not ready for?"

"Eric, we've been over this. I've seen how you interact with women. Your attention is fleeting at best, caustic at worst. Why would I sign myself up for that?"

"Has it ever occurred to you that maybe I haven't met the right girl? I went after the one I wanted most, and you wrote me off like I'm not even worth consideration. What am I supposed to do? My nights may be filled with strange, but at least I'm not stuck in a relationship with someone who bores me half to death. You on the other hand—"

Thunk! She just chucked the kitchen plate into the sink. *Shit.*

"I'm done with this conversation."

"Of course you are," I mutter.

"Quit picking a fight. That's not the reason I came here tonight."

"Could've fooled me."

She rubs her temples and sighs heavily. "Can we just stick to the original plan? Keep things drama-free for once?"

Ambitious, given how we operate. "Fine. If you're done eating, get over here and pick your colors."

"No. Not if you're going to act like a dick."

I strike my fist against the table. "Dammit, Rave. What do you want from me?"

"Your attention. Is that too much to ask?"

She wants a distraction, someone to take her mind off her problems. I can relate, but she picked the wrong guy. If she wanted compliant, she should've gone to Brandon's. But she came here instead. Why? Because deep down, she knows I won't give her what she wants; I'll give her what she needs. And there lies the key difference between Brandon and me.

My lungs deflate. "Come here."

She stays put and studies me. Not entirely sure what she's looking for, but I doubt she'll find it. Even if I were offering up my emotions like dirty little secrets, she wouldn't learn anything new. I'd make damn sure of that. I hold up her coffee mug in one hand and a paintbrush in the other. "Truce?"

A reluctant smile escapes. She walks over and grabs both items out of my hands, then rounds the table to stand directly across from me. Our gazes collide. Soft tension erupts. I'm suddenly unable to remember what we were even arguing about in the first place.

"Can we please not talk about Brandon anymore?" she says.

Ah, memory jogged. "Who's Brandon?"

There's the smile I've been waiting for.

No more digs at her relationship, I tell myself. She needs a friend right now. "I'm sorry for being an ass."

"Same here."

No matter how hard I try, I can't quit this girl. As much as I want to talk about us, it's better if we don't. She's not in the right headspace for it and I don't want to make her feel uncomfortable. I'll simply bide my time until she breaks up with Brandon. It's bound to happen sooner or later. Right?

Four Years Ago....

"Tell me about her," Vivienne prompts.

I shovel a spoonful of Ramen into my mouth and stall. She taps the end of her pen against my manila file, reading me like a book.

"What do you wanna know?"

26

"Whatever you're willing to share."

"She's my neighbor. We've painted together a few times."

"Not graffiti, I hope."

"Nope. You'd be proud. I've been staying out of trouble recently."

"Good. Is she a senior, too?"

"No."

She's waiting....

"She's a freshman."

I don't normally offer up so much information, but I can't hold it in any longer. I need to talk to someone about this. Every time I broach the subject with my buddy Chase Williams, one of the three non-douchebags at my new school, he warns me not to go there. He insists Andre would beat my ass if he saw me hanging around his little sister. And he has a point.

"I see," Vivienne nods. "Do you like her as a friend, or more?"

"Both. But I refuse to make a move. She's too young."

"Do you think you can stick to that?"

"I don't have a choice. If she were a couple years older, I'd be all over her, but I'm not looking for jailbait. That's just asking for trouble. Especially when you factor in my probation."

"I think that's a wise decision, Eric."

"You'd like her though. She's a good girl." *Why am I seeking her approval? Cut that out.*

"I'm sure I would," she smiles reassuringly. Her gaze drops to her notes. "While we're on the subject, have you given any thought to what I said about Levi?"

Not one bit.

"I have," I lie, "but I'm not changing my mind. We may not hang out as much because of the move, but I'm not dropping him. He's not as bad as you think."

"No, Eric. *You're* not as bad as you think."

I stiffen. Where the hell did that come from? I swallow my insecurity, feeling the air around us thicken with tension. It's sobering. My natural instinct is to bolt or deflect. I lean forward and place the bowl of Ramen on the coffee table, avoiding eye contact at all costs. "Do me a favor and hold the judgment till noon."

"I'm not judging you. I'm simply tossing a theory out there."

"Which is?"

"Has it ever occurred to you that maybe the reason you take the fall for Levi is because you think you deserve to be punished for something? Or perhaps you feel like you don't deserve anything good in your life?"

Silence.

"Would you say there's any truth to either of those assessments?"

I lean forward and glare. "What's your angle?"

She's unfazed by my hostility. "Why do you always assume I have hidden motives? I'm not your enemy, Eric. I'm trying to help you. But I can't help if you won't let me."

"What do you want from me?"

"I want you to be able to move forward and let go of your past so you can heal. You deserve to find some semblance of peace and happiness."

"I've moved on. It's buried. There's nothing more to say."

She studies me. "Eric, you haven't worked through your issues. We can sit here and talk about the light and easy stuff all day, but it's not going to get you to where you want to be. You need to be willing to open up more. At least give me something."

My chest is rising and falling rapidly. Clever bitch trapped me. It's a double-edged sword. If I get up and walk away, she wins. If I give in and spill my guts, she still wins.

"Tell me about your parents," she presses.

"No. Next."

She sets her pen down and waits for me to elaborate. It's obvious she's not going to budge. I check my phone to see how much time we have left. Thirty-two minutes. Shit. I'm royally screwed. Fight the inevitable for as long as possible. If I'm going down, I'm going down swinging. This tactic lasts a whopping four minutes.

"My parents. They're both living their own separate lives."

"And how does that make you feel? Knowing they're out there but making no real effort to contact you?"

"How do you think that makes me feel?"

"You tell me."

My fists ball up. "It makes me feel like shit, okay? There. Is that what you want to hear?" Why am I allowing this woman to cut me? Maybe she's right. Maybe I am a glutton for punishment.

"How old were you when they split up?"

"I don't know, five? They were on-and-off for a while after that, then Dad ditched us for good a few years later."

"Why'd he leave?"

"He couldn't handle my mom." *And my mom couldn't handle me. And I can't handle this.* I feel claustrophobic on the inside. Is that even possible?

"What do you mean by that?"

"She was young. It wasn't her fault."

"What wasn't her fault?"

"My dad leaving. He knew what he was getting himself into. He knew she had a kid and a bunch of other baggage."

"Do you hold him responsible for everything?"

"I hold him responsible for his fair share. He gave up when Mom and I needed him the most. You don't get to just walk away after you committed to helping raise a child you knew wasn't yours. When things were solid, he had no problem claiming me as his own, but when shit hit the fan with my mom, he couldn't distance himself from me fast enough."

"That must've been hard. When was the last time you saw him?"

"I don't know. Ten years ago. Why?"

"Where do you think he lives now?"

"Fuck if I know. Probably on a beach somewhere. Or maybe he's living the whole white picket fence, suburbia bullshit. I'm sure he married some Stepford Wife type along the way who gave him 2.5 overachieving children, and they all sit down around the table at dinnertime, sharing stories and holding hands and praying."

"What's the last memory you have of him?"

I must get off on this—torturing myself. I cave and describe in vivid detail—down to the very outfit he was wearing—the last time I saw my dad. How he screamed at my mom at the top of his lungs. How I sat at our kitchen table plugging my ears, desperately trying to drown out the fighting. How he grabbed his keys and his wallet, said he was done with us, and slammed the door so hard a picture fell off the wall. I'll never forget the sound of his truck as it roared to life, gravel crunching beneath the tires. I ran over to the window with tears streaming down my face, and that was it. He didn't even come back for the rest of his stuff. No phone calls, no visitations, no birthday cards.

Nothing.

Vivienne leans back. "Now we're getting somewhere."

After she sucks the last scraps of my soul out of my chest, we call it quits. Actually, first she says I have serious abandonment issues and need to work on trusting people without pushing them away, then she seals fragments of my soul in a Mason jar. And she does it with a smug smile.

She knows too much, which officially makes her a threat.

My conclusion: I can no longer trust her.

My next conclusion: she's gotta go.

Unbeknownst to Viv, this is our last session.

FOUR

r a v e n

"Get your ass in the pool, Raven!" Emilio commands. "Or I'll throw you in."

"She doesn't want to get her hair wet," Tori informs. She's lounging in a hot pink bikini, soakin' up what's left of the sun's rays. Her newest addiction is tanning. The girl has no self-control. The second she starts looking like one of those idiots from *Jersey Shore*, I'm cutting her off.

I smile widely and look around, taking in the scene. I'm surrounded by amazing friends, fabulous weather—having the time of my life. Tori and I invited some people over to check out our brand-new apartment. Eric and Emilio were sweet enough to haul all the boxes and furniture up, then we all hit the pool to cool down.

It's a day full of celebrations: Mia's back for the summer, Tori and I both got accepted into UT in the fall, and today's my eighteenth birthday.

And they say youth is wasted on the young.

Eric breaks the surface of the water next to my pool chair, slicks his blond hair back. He's been working out like crazy with all the lawn care and landscaping jobs, and it shows. Water trickles down and falls off his body like a slow motion ad for Cool Water cologne. Utterly ridiculous. He's filled out in all the right areas, leaving no trace of the teenager he once was.

"Anyone up for grilling tonight?" he looks around to gauge potential takers.

"You don't have to ask me twice," Mia answers, slipping her sunglasses over her eyes and sitting down by the edge of the pool to dip her feet in the water.

"That's the spirit!"

Eric swims over and grabs her by the waist. Before she can even process what's happening, he launches her into the pool. She manages to scream before impact.

Emilio laughs hysterically.

Mia resurfaces and coughs up a mouthful of water. "Dammit, Eric!"

"Sorry, Strawberry. Couldn't help myself. You got me all excited."

She flips him off.

Ever since I introduced them a few years ago, they've developed the most twisted friendship. We've all become inseparable. The downside: Mia can relate to him in ways I can't. They're not into each other like that, but they're extremely flirty. It's annoying. To her credit, she has no idea how I feel about him.

"What about you, birthday girl?" Eric asks, tugging me out of my own head. He's looking at me expectantly, waiting for my answer. Beneath the surface, he's waiting for something else entirely.

"Grilling sounds good. Do y'all want to run to the store and pick up stuff while us girls start unpacking?"

"We can do that." He turns to look at Emilio. "You ready, man? I'll buy if you drive."

"Deal." Emilio hoists himself out of the pool.

Eric follows suit.

"Do you guys mind picking up some booze while you're out?" Mia asks, floating weightlessly on her back.

He glances down at her. "You know, just for asking that question I'm going to pick you up some milk."

"Make sure it's chocolate."

"I'll make sure it's whole," he guarantees.

"Doubt it. You wouldn't know wholesome if it sat on your face."

"Wanna bet?" he says, looking like he might jump back in.

Mia splashes water at him and submerges herself before he has a chance to dive back in and tackle her. She swims to the edge, boosts herself up, wrings her long dark hair out, and flips it over her shoulder. Eric and Emilio grab towels and dry themselves off. I tear my eyes off Eric's body and get a grip before I feel the need to jump in the pool and cool down too.

"Looks like I'm late to the party," a familiar voice calls out, hosing down my hormones. Brandon closes the gate behind him and strides over carrying a gift. Once he reaches us, he bends down and plants a kiss on my cheek. "Happy Birthday, baby."

He hands me the present. Accepting this knowing I have feelings for someone else doesn't feel right in my gut. But Brandon's good for me. I couldn't ask for a better guy. So why am I not feeling it? Where's the disjoint? Why is this so confusing?

It's becoming clear that this exchange is making everyone visibly uncomfortable. The tension is palpable. Eric's staring at Brandon like he's an imposter.

"Thank you, babe," I say.

"What are you waiting for? Go ahead and open it."

Not wanting to make this more awkward, I tear apart the wrapping paper. It's a tiny black box holding a pair of silver, heart-shaped earrings inside. I swallow past the lump clogging my throat.

"They're beautiful."

Out of my periphery, I notice Eric tense up.

"Do you not like them?" Brandon asks, assessing my reaction.

"No, no. They're perfect." I kiss him square on the lips, hoping to dispel his suspicions.

He caresses my face and deepens the kiss, then pulls back. "I just want to make you happy. You know that, right?"

I swallow and nod. Eric and Emilio slip their shirts on and leave.

"Where're they headed?" Brandon asks.

"To grab some food."

"So...you already have dinner plans?"

"Yeah, the boys want to grill. But you're welcome to stay."

He forces a smile to appear. "I'd love to. Can I steal you away tomorrow night for a belated birthday dinner?"

"Sure. I already asked for the weekend off, so I'm in the clear."

I hate myself for making another promise, but I can't seem to find the right time or the courage to end this thing. Events and people keep getting in the way. And I refuse to break up with him on my birthday. I want to have fun with my friends, not break someone's heart. On the flipside, he doesn't deserve to be strung along, either.

"Can I see your apartment?" he asks.

"Yeah." I stand up and grab my stuff. "We were just heading up to unpack."

After I give Brandon the grand tour, we spend the next fifteen minutes rearranging furniture and unpacking boxes. My friends are my superheroes. They always come through. We divide and conquer, each tackling separate rooms. Plus, they've come up to help so that I'm not alone with Brandon—whether that was intentional or not, doesn't even matter. They're even awesome when they're not trying. I'm in the kitchen putting away all the dishes when Eric and Emilio waltz through the front door.

"We humble servants come bearing gifts," Eric announces, setting the grocery bags and beer on the countertop. He lets out a heavy breath and fishes his phone out of his pocket to respond to a text. Probably some girl he met in the booze aisle. I distract myself by unloading everything. Emilio disappears into the bathroom.

"I wouldn't use humble or servant to describe you."

He stops texting and looks up at me. "Well, it certainly wouldn't be used to describe you, either."

I grab the brats and toss them at his chest. "Feed me."

"Why should I?"

"Because I'm the birthday girl."

He tosses the brats aside, checks the hall to make sure no one's watching, then grips the edge of the counter and leans over so our faces are inches apart.

The playful vibe shifts.

As Mia would say, "Shit just got real."

"Back up," I order.

"You're going to have to do better than that," he says.

My heart rate spikes.

"What are you doing? Brandon is right down the hall." I try to keep my voice even, but my nerves are piqued. We're not technically crossing any lines, but if someone walked in and saw us, we'd definitely be giving the wrong impression.

His gaze is steady, intense—like he's desperately trying to convey something. "As if that would stop me. He doesn't make you happy."

We're sliding into dangerous territory.

"…And you know this how?"

"Because I never see you look at him this way."

"Like how?" I push.

His gaze drops to my mouth, then it travels back up my face.

"Like you want me to defile you."

I swallow thickly. The sexual tension that's been boiling to the brim for years just spilled over. This is pure torture. I want nothing more than to give in—right here, right now. I want to grab his gorgeous face and kiss him so hard—make him forget about all those other nameless girls and leave a lasting impact. This is what Brandon and I are missing. Passion. Chemistry.

Just go for it, stupid.

I inch forward, part my lips, and let my gaze slip to his mouth. As I'm about to seal the deal, the toilet flushes, the bathroom door swings open, heavy footprints creep closer to the kitchen. I jump back several paces because nothing screams "innocent" like plenty of physical distance.

Emilio rounds the corner to the kitchen, stops mid-stride. His eyes dart back and forth between Eric and me. "Am I interrupting something?"

"Not at all," Eric lies. He reaches for the brats, the bag of coals, and the lighter, then looks back at Emilio like nothing ever happened. "You ready?"

"Yeah, just give me a minute. I'll bring the rest of the stuff down," Emilio says, unsure of how to react.

Eric nods and glances in my direction, his lips pull up into a flirtatious smile. In a flash, he's gone.

Emilio closes the distance between us. "What's the matter with you, huh? Are you trying to get caught?"

"No. I'm trying to figure out what I want."

"Then take the time to do that, but don't play games."

"I'm not."

He grabs the tongs, a couple beers, and heads for the door.

"Emilio?"

He freezes but doesn't turn around.

"Please don't say anything to Eric, or to Brand—"

He turns and stares. "You're my sister. I'm on your side no matter what. But don't be stupid." And with that, he's gone.

Silence fills the room. My elbows meet the counter with a light thud as I bury my head in my hands, exhaling my frustration. Why is this so complicated? Must I have to be the one to hurt Brandon? Isn't he sick of me yet?

Ugh, FML!

An incoming text yanks me out of my momentary slump. I reach for my phone, secretly hoping it's Eric.

Tori: *Boy problems?*

How'd she know that?

The floor creaks and my head snaps up. I find Tori standing near the edge of the hallway, watching my live freak out like it's a Broadway show. I zip around the counter, grab her by the hand, and drag her out to the balcony. Once we're outside and out of earshot, I take a deep breath and tell her, "We have a problem."

"Spill."

"It's Emilio; he caught us."

"Caught who? You and Eric?"

I nod.

"Doing what, exactly?"

"Nothing like that. Well, kinda. I don't know. We were in the kitchen talking—"

"And by talking you mean flirting," she interjects.

"Right. One minute everything was fine, and then the next he got up close and personal. I can't think straight when he does that." By this point, I'm pacing.

"And then I thought to myself, 'Gee, he might make a stellar boyfriend. He understands me better than anyone, he puts up with my antics, knows exactly what to say to make me laugh, and most importantly, he lets me rewind all my favorite parts as many times as I want during Thursday Movie Nights.'"

"That's important?"

"Extremely. Not many people have the patience. It's the small things. I want him, Tori. God, I want him like crazy. But is he the right choice? I don't want to give up a guy who treats me well for one who doesn't. Eric loves being single. Can he handle a committed relationship? Is he capable of being a loyal boyfriend? These are the thoughts that plague my mind. If one of us makes a move and it doesn't turn out the way we planned, we'll lose everything. He's seen me at my best and loved me at my worst. We accept each other exactly for who we are, flaws and all. Dating him changes those dynamics. Why put my heart out on the line and risk it all for something that's potentially less transparent and authentic than what I already have?"

"I get that, but where does Emilio come in during all this?"

"He walked in on us when we were seconds away from kissing."

"Oh, shit."

I stop pacing and plant my hands on my hips. "Yeah."

"Personally, I think you need to cut the cord with Brandon and be done with it. Then take some space and see how you feel about the whole Eric situation. Maybe you'll have a better grasp on what you want. You can always try talking to Mia, too," she suggests.

"No way. I don't want her caught in the middle. She's just as close to Eric as I am. I'm not putting her in the position where she's forced to take sides. As soon as I figure everything out, I'll fill her in. Until then, she needs to remain blissfully unaware and neutral. Switzerland."

"Speaking of Mia," Tori clears her throat.

I spin around. The door to the balcony opens up and Mia pokes her head out, her hazel eyes analyzing the situation. She slips her body through and closes the door. "What are you ho-bags doing out here?"

"Figuring out the best way for Raven to break up with Brandon," Tori covers.

The surprise on Mia's face is quickly replaced by sympathy. "Oh, no. What happened?"

"I can't do it anymore, Mia. He doesn't make me feel anything out of the ordinary. There's no rush of emotion. No excitement. The relationship should be fresh and fun. I shouldn't have to try and force a connection with him or convince myself he's the right choice. If he were, I'd feel it. And if we don't have it by now, we're not gonna get it. God, I suck. He's mapping out our future, and I'm searching for the emergency exit."

"You're not feelin' it. There's nothing wrong with that. At the end of the day, all that matters is whether or not you're happy in the relationship. Clearly you're not, so he's gotta go," Mia answers, sliding her hand across her throat to represent Brandon's demise.

Tori points to Mia. "What she said."

"But what should I say to him?"

"Just tell him the truth and try to let him down easy," Mia suggests.

I take a deep breath and brace myself. I can't deal with this awful feeling anymore. Forget what I said earlier about not wanting to break his heart on my birthday. I have no choice. The longer I wait, the worse this will become. And I can't bear the thought of having the word *cheater* plastered onto my guilty conscience. I can barely tolerate *heartbreaker,* but at least by sparing him more pain, hopefully, he'll be able to forgive me for what I'm about to do.

I walk into my room to find Brandon unpacking my boxes and categorizing my stuff because he knows that's how I like it. Wish he would stop being so great for once. It would make my job easier. "Hey, can we talk outside for a minute?" I ask timidly, leaning my hip against the dresser. My confidence is nowhere to be found.

"Sure. What's up?"

I motion my head toward the front door, urging him to follow. As soon as we hit the hallway, my friends scatter like roaches and pretend to be busy doing something moderately important. Brandon's used to their weird behavior at this point. He opens the front door and ushers me out—a true gentleman until the end.

Once we make it down to the parking lot, I suggest going to his car for some privacy. Getting dumped sucks. No need to throw salt on the wound by allowing bystanders to witness it.

Once we climb inside, he asks, "What's going on?" There's an edge of nervousness to his voice.

Be brave and honest. Be brave and honest, I chant in my head.

"Tell me something you can't stand about me."

My request catches him off guard. He shifts around in his seat, clearly uncomfortable. "Uh...is this some kind of test?"

I adjust my body so I'm facing him. "No, it's not. Tell me something about my personality that drives you crazy."

His response is so instantaneous you'd think it was queued up. "Not a thing. You're perfect."

Liar!

He grasps my chin and strokes the side of my cheek with his thumb. I close my eyes and relish the feeling one last time. I'm about to break his heart, and he's the one comforting me. How messed up is that?

I reopen my eyes and use them to summon the truth out of him. "Be honest."

I can't explain why, but I need this. Maybe it's to make myself feel better for what's about to happen. Maybe it's because I deserve to suffer. Or maybe it's because deep down I'm searching for something more, something real.

He releases my chin and rests one hand on top of the steering wheel and stares out the windshield, lost in thought. While his gaze is fixated on something else, mine is still fixated solely on him. Several beats pass. Finally, he looks over. There's a sadness in his eyes that wasn't there before.

"Why are you doing this?"

"Doing what?"

"Trying to pick a fight with me on your birthday."

"I'm not. I'm trying to get you to tell the truth."

"By hurting you," he says, confused.

I look down and fumble around with the hem of my shorts, searching for the right words. There aren't any. There's nothing I can say or do to make this easier.

"Look, Brandon, you are by far one of the sweetest guys I've ever known—"

"But…" he presses, starting to see where this is going.

"And you've been so good to me." I let that one linger. I never want him to think things could've turned out differently had he treated me better. The reality is, I couldn't have asked for a more thoughtful, attentive boyfriend. It just wasn't in the cards for us. That's nobody's fault. Although, it sure feels like mine right now.

"Spit it out, Raven."

I flinch at his harsh tone. A lone tear escapes and falls down my cheek. I wipe it away with the back of my hand. When I finally work up the courage to look him straight in the eyes again, I crumble. "I'm so sorry. Please don't hate me."

His hands grip the steering wheel tightly, making the veins under his skin bulge. "Are you seriously breaking up with me? On your birthday? In my car?"

More tears fall. I nod, compounded with heaps of guilt.

"Are you at least going to give me a reason why?"

I take a calming breath and force myself to form a coherent sentence. He deserves an explanation. He deserves a lot more than that, but I can't be the one to give it to him. "I like you, Brandon, but as a friend. This isn't working anymore."

He glares at me. "Wow, really? That's news to me. So things aren't perfect for two fucking seconds and you decide to kick me to the curb like yesterday's trash? You don't even bother to give me a chance to fix it first? Jesus, Raven." He runs his hands through his hair, considering his next words. "You're so selfish sometimes. You only care about yourself and anything that benefits you." He shakes his head like he doesn't understand what he ever saw in me. That's the sharpest blade of them all.

I stay silent, processing his coarse words, unsure of what to say or do next. I didn't expect things to go this way. I knew it wouldn't be smooth, but I never thought he'd lash out at me in retaliation. Yes, he's upset and hurt, but so am I. Does he seriously think I wanted to hurt him on purpose? That's the last thing I ever intended. Luckily, I don't have to ponder any of this for long.

"Please get out of my car," he says with an air of finality. He starts the engine and leans back against the seat, anxiously waiting for me to leave.

I reach down into my pocket and fish out the earrings he gave me. I open the glove compartment and place them inside.

"Just keep them."

I ignore his comment and close the compartment. I turn to grab the handle and pause, looking back over my shoulder at him one last time. "I really am sorry," I whisper, opening the door and stepping out. As soon as I shut the door, he reverses and hightails it out of the parking lot, leaving an imaginary trail of dust behind, and a not-so-imaginary birthday girl in tears.

FIVE

e r i c

"Where's Raven?" I ask, scanning the living room. My gaze settles on two wide-eyed faces: Tori and Mia. They're sitting together on the couch, watching the front door like hawks. Tori's biting her nails and Mia's knee is bouncing up and down restlessly. They're acting like a couple of tweakers on standby.

Something's up.

Without bothering to take her eyes off the door, Mia answers. "She's outside."

"We just came from outside and we didn't see her."

Emilio grabs a brat off the plate I'm holding and walks over to the counter to grab a bun and some Dijon mustard, oblivious to what's happening in Girl World.

"That's because she went out front to break up with Brandon," Tori explains, then she takes a cue from Emilio and stands up and walks over to grab a brat.

She's breaking up with him?

"How long ago?"

Tori shrugs. "I don't know, fifteen minutes?"

Without thinking, I shove the plate into her unsteady arms and leave to go find Raven.

"Hey! Warn me next time before you do that!"

The door closes behind me. I ignore Tori's comment and take the stairs two at a time until I reach the pavement. Raven's car is still parked in its designated spot. I look around for Brandon's car, but it's nowhere in sight.

Shit. Maybe she left with him?

No. She wouldn't leave without telling one of us.

The sound of sniffling beckons my attention. I look over to find Raven sitting on the grass underneath a tree. She's hugging her knees to her chest protectively, crying. Christ. The drama. Everything's life or death with this girl. I'm relieved she broke it off with What's His Face, though. They were a wrong fit from the start. The guy can't hang. I tried to tell her that several times, but did she listen? Of course not.

I'll bet he can't even name her favorite book. It's *Little Women,* by the way. Favorite movie? *Breakfast at Tiffany's.*

Her newest crisis is feeling torn between majoring in what's practical and chasing her dreams as far as they'll take her. She hates uncertainty but loves surprises. Those tidbits will get you VIP status.

What about her fears? Does he know she's deathly afraid of cockroaches and the concept of thrift shopping? I can't get her anywhere near a Goodwill or Salvation Army. She'll hyperventilate. No, that doesn't mean she's shallow. She's just more honest about her phobias than most.

When she's upset, she organizes anything and everything she can get her hands on. That's why she's banned from my kitchen cupboards, my paint collection, and my closet. I can never find anything after she's done.

I guess love is similar to art in that regard. It's picking up on the small, seemingly insignificant aspects. Paying close attention to things that most people skip over and don't think twice about. An eye for detail. That's what separates me from the rest of the pack. I'm not saying I'm worthy of her. Who am I kidding? What can I offer? She deserves to live in a castle, and all I can give her is a shack. It would be colorful and nicely decorated, though. Original artwork.

But back to the crying thing. I can't stand to watch her cry. I sigh and walk over there, on a mission to make it all better.

"What happened?"

She lifts her head, surprised to see me. Black mascara streaks are running down her cheeks, and her eyes are all red and puffy.

I shove both hands into my pockets and shuffle my feet back and forth, scuffing my paint-splattered Timbs. I'm not good with sadness. Or coming up with the right thing to say. But if I don't pipe in, this level of discomfort is going to become unbearable. Neither of us wants that. I pull myself together. "Let me rephrase. Why the fuck are you crying on your birthday?"

"I broke up with Brandon. He kicked me out of his car and took off."

"Sooo...he took it well?" I deadpan.

She rolls her raccoon eyes and kicks me so hard in the shin I double over.

"Dammit, woman! Get a grip!"

She stands up and brushes the dirt off her butt. "This is all your fault!"

"How is this my fault?"

"You were the one who told me I wasn't happy with him."

"Because you weren't."

"That's none of your business!" she shrieks.

Time out. Can somebody throw me a pair of earmuffs? In between shin rubs, I have to keep reminding myself not to put my hands on her, despite the overwhelming urge to wrap my fingers around her neck and throttle her. "You made it my business. You made it everyone's business when you ran around and whined about how unhappy you were."

Judging by the expression on her face, I've gone too far. She's about to freeze me out or go thermonuclear. I'm not sure which is worse.

I take a step back and run my hands through my hair, bracing myself for the storm. I've yet to meet anyone who riles me up more than Raven. We bring out the best in each other. And the absolute worst. That's the problem with catching feelings. Sometimes it happens so suddenly, before you even realize what's going on, you've become a different person—someone you barely recognize. Different isn't always better, either. I witnessed that firsthand with my parents.

"All right! I get it! I'm a horrible person. I only care about myself and anything that revolves around me. I'm sorry I burdened y'all. Here I thought I was leaning on my friends for moral support. I'm sorry you find me so difficult to deal with. I'm sorry I'm so high-maintenance. I'm sorry I have no redeeming qualities. There. Have I said it all? If not, spare me the tirade. Brandon already beat you to the punch fifteen minutes ago."

I was about to apologize for the low blow, but this…well, I've lost my train of thought. "He said all that to you?"

"More or less," she mutters dejectedly. She crosses her arms over her chest. "He told me I was selfish for not giving him a chance to fix the relationship."

She turns and saunters across the parking lot, a move I'm all too familiar with. Why does she always do that? Translation: she's over it. I refrain from chasing her down. I need to chill out and give her space to clear her head.

I keep an eye on her from a distance. She lays down on the hood of my car in the beating sun and stares up at the powder blue sky. Watching her like this reminds me of when we were neighbors. There were nights when I'd roll in from a late-night graffiti session and catch her stargazing outside in her hammock. I spent more time than I'd care to admit trying to figure out what was on her mind. Was she thinking about me? Did she know her very presence was my sole motivation for getting up early and going to school every day? I don't think I've ever told her that. Randomly seeing her face in the halls made it worth the endless hours of boredom and detention stints.

The better part of me refuses to let that very same girl be upset on her birthday. I snap out of it and jog across the parking lot. When I reach my car, my butt slides against the hood and makes a loud farting noise. I stiffen. One second goes by…two…three. I risk taking a peek at her.

"That wasn't me."

She can barely keep a straight face.

What a way to break the ice.

I lean back against the windshield, crossing my feet at the ankles. One arm slips behind my head. Even though we're lying side by side, she's a million miles away. I reach down to touch her hand, determined to bring her back. When my palm grazes her skin, she unexpectedly flips her hand over and interlaces our fingers. I exhale a sigh of disbelief…and relief.

It feels natural to hold her hand—along with scary, exciting, and intimate. It's the first time she's ever let me touch her this way. Probably the last. What happened in the kitchen earlier doesn't count. We weren't touching. That was pretty incredible in itself, though. But I have to keep reminding myself that her judgment is clouded.

As much as I want to take whatever this is between us further, I'm well aware that putting the moves on a girl less than twenty-four hours after a breakup is a big no-no—even for me. Then again, we all know how I feel about boundaries. If her guilt weren't holding the situation hostage, I'd probably go for it. *Has it even been twenty-four minutes?*

"For the record, letting go of someone when you're unhappy may seem like the selfish choice, but it makes you merciful in the long run. Nobody wants to be caged, least of all you. Never apologize for that. Besides, it's not like you were married with kids 'n shit."

"Tell that to Brandon," she mutters.

"Fuck that guy. He doesn't even know the first thing about you. Never did. And I can tell you where you went wrong in this whole situation."

"Oh, really? Enlighten me."

"Where was his latte? His home cooked breakfast? Did those things ever even cross your mind before jumping in his car? Shame on you. I taught you better. Bad grasshopper." I throw in a Mr. Miyagi accent for kicks—no pun intended.

She props herself up on her elbows. "Are you being serious?"

It doesn't go unnoticed that she's still holding my hand.

"Don't knock the method. It works like a charm. People always handle a breakup better on a full stomach, especially guys. We're so needy."

She throws her head back in exasperation. "Oh, my God. The clinginess level is suffocating."

"It's pitiful."

"And so unattractive."

"But secretly a little endearing."

I'm rewarded with the sound of her laugh. I squeeze her hand and hop off the car.

"Come on. Everyone's probably wondering if we're still alive. You need to eat and get ready for the surprise. I'm saving mine for Thursday Movie Night when it's just you and me. And FYI, we'll be watching *The Big Lebowski*. It's my pick this week, remember?"

Her eyes widen with excitement. "Will there be presents?"

"Among other things."

She rolls off the car ninja-style, then bends down to check her reflection in my side mirror and gasps at the gruesome sight.

I open the passenger's door and grab a spare tee out of the front seat. "Here," I toss it over the roof.

She holds it out in front and inspects it closely. "Gross. Is this a used gym shirt?"

"No, but it's been sitting in my car for over a month, so enjoy."

She brings it in close and hesitates before taking a whiff.

"See? Told you it wasn't a gym shirt."

Her eyes search my face to see if I'm lying. When she's convinced I'm not, she uses the hem to meticulously wipe under her eyes. Once we overcome that massive hurdle, she moves on to scrub her cheeks. Tackling one world-ending issue at a time today.

"Rave, speed it up. We've got places to be and people to see."

She throws my now mascara-smudged tee at my chest with a handful of attitude. I use each end to swirl the shirt around until it's twisted tight like a rope. I round the car and take my aim.

She backs up. "Don't you dare."

When I charge, she bolts.

I chase her around the parking lot until she's within lashing distance. When I have a clear shot, I seize the opportunity and snap the shirt right on her tight ass.

"*Ouch!*" she screams, rubbing her backside. "What the hell!"

"That's for kicking me in the shin."

"Next time I'll aim higher," she threatens.

"It'll be your funeral."

I drape the tee over my shoulder and walk back to the apartment, not bothering to wait up. Ten steps later, Raven barrels into my side. I wrap my arm around her neck and casually pull her in. This is the safest method. It's all about mastering the art of being near someone without letting them get too close. Keeping them at arm's length. Until she's in the right frame of mind and gives me a clear sign she wants more, that's where she'll stay. I've spent enough effort expressing my desires over the last year only to be shot down. A person can only take so much rejection.

"Where are we going tonight?" she asks.

"No clue. Tori and Mia planned everything. Your brother and I are just tagging along for the ride. Better be somewhere good."

What the fuck?

Those are the only three words I can conjure up to accurately describe my reaction. Why didn't I see this coming? What bizarre, alternate reality have I landed in? Looking back, the signs were all there. Glitter on the floor, dim lighting, and two enticing poles residing on either side of the stage. My thoughts immediately drifted to strip club. It was a brief twenty seconds where I thought all of my wildest fantasies were coming together in one beautiful, wet dream come true. Me, Rave, and two other gorgeous women all partying it up in a strip joint. Sounds like heaven, right? Minus Emilio imposing as the fifth wheel, of course. That part I could do without. But seriously. I was about to pull out my Washingtons and make it rain.

The idea wasn't far-fetched. Raven did just turn eighteen. And what better way to celebrate? I should've trusted my instincts when they told me something weird was going on. For instance, why wouldn't Tori and Mia tell us where we were all going? Where were the exotic dancers? And why the lack of men? It's Friday night. Ideally, this place should be packed.

Now it all makes sense. I guess that's where the joke's on me, because nothing could've prepared me for the moment when my eyes settled on the stage and a transvestite named Coco Butter took the entire club by storm in a shiny dress, black wig, and nearly a pound of makeup.

And here we are. Back to the present. How on earth do I continuously get roped into these situations? If I'm not helping Mia pick out bras, buying chocolate ice cream for Tori during "Aunt

Flow's" monthly visit (I refuse to pick up tampons for someone who isn't my girlfriend, and yes, in case you're wondering, she's asked), and still trying to retain some semblance of masculinity, then I'm here. At a drag show.

Again, WTF?

Coco grabs the mic and flips her hair over one shoulder.

"Ladies and Gays, welcome to the show! Up first we have the fabulous Miss Ruby Redd performing "I Kissed A Girl" by Katy Perry. Let's give it up for Miss Ruby Redd!"

The estrogen-heavy crowd goes nuts—no pun. I glance over at Emilio and shake my head and shrug in disbelief. It's all I can do at this point. He mirrors my actions.

I whip out my phone and text Mia and Tori the exact same message: *I hope a colony of fire ants infest your vagina while you're sleeping. Also, I'm drinking all your beer tonight. Go find someone else to be your errand boy.*

I slip my phone back into my pocket. Ruby Redd has started making rounds, grabbing tips from various customers. Who knew you're supposed to tip a drag queen? Tori, Mia, and Raven all pull out singles and raise them up high, dancing in their seats while they wait. Thank God I can legally drink. I remove myself and make a beeline for the bar.

A man dressed like Marilyn Monroe hands the customer in front her drink. Raven would be giddy over the fact that Marilyn is serving drinks. I recognize the dress from *The Seven Year Itch*—one of the many of old movies she's forced me to sit through. The things I do for that girl.

Marilyn eyes me up and down. "What can I get you, handsome?"

"Uh, a gin and tonic, please."

"Can I see your ID?"

I flash my driver's license.

"One gin and tonic comin' right up."

I sift through my wallet and pull out a five and some ones. Might as well use the Washingtons on the bartender. I'm gonna be smashed by the time this is all over. As Marilyn pours my drink, my phone vibrates.

Mia: *So tell me, what should I do when I get that burning sensation? You're the expert.*

Smartass.

Me: *I may be a slut, but I'm a clean one. Can you say the same for yourself?*

Mia: *Of course. After all, my track record is better than yours.*

Me: *And how would you know?*

Mia: *Girls talk.*

Me: *Really? All the way in Kansas? Because that's where you live nine months out of the year and I don't recall ever fucking anyone from out of state. I like my pussy local. Good try, though.*

Mia: *Whatever. Enjoy the show because you're gonna be here for another two hours. Cheers!*

Me: *Funny, I keep rereading that last text but all I see is defeat, defeat, defeat.*

My suspicions are confirmed when she doesn't reply. What can I say? Some people can't hang. When I look back up, Marilyn is watching me intently with one hand perched on her hip.

I slap the cash down and grab my drink. But before I can walk away—

"You don't come here often, do you?" she inquires.

"What gave me away?"

"Who are you here with?"

What's with the game of twenty-one questions? I point in the direction of our table. "I'm with them. It's my friend's eighteenth birthday."

"Which one?"

"The girl in the plum colored dress."

"She's pretty."

"She's stunning," I correct.

Marilyn smiles and winks. "Enjoy the drink, honey. And relax. We don't bite."

I smile back and raise my glass. "Thanks for this."

"My pleasure."

I take a sip and saunter back over to our table. The girls are all singing at the top of their lungs. When I pull up a seat, Emilio eyes the drink in my hand. "Dude, you couldn't wait?"

"Nope."

He leans in so I can hear him over the music. "We need an escape plan, ASAP."

"I'm working on it."

He nods and leans back.

"What are y'all talking about over there?" Tori yells over the table.

"Prostate exams," I shout back.

A look of pure disgust paints her face. It's comedic. Makes me remember the text I sent a few minutes ago. "Hey, check your phone."

I fold my arms over my chest and lean back against the chair with a shit-eating grin spread across my face. Tori opens up her clutch and pulls her phone out. As soon as she reads the message, I receive the death stare.

Eric: 1

Tori: 0

When the first performance ends, Coco reappears to make an announcement. "All right, y'all. Give it up one last time for Miss Ruby Redd!"

We all oblige.

Coco continues. "We've just been informed that there's a birthday girl in the house tonight. Where's she at?"

Raven stiffens and glances at Tori and Mia, no doubt believing they're the culprits. They shake their heads simultaneously.

"Stand up, birthday girl," Coco orders.

Raven takes a quick inventory of everyone in the club and stands up on shaky legs. She adjusts the bottom of her dress and raises her hand. "Over here."

Coco's gaze finds Raven. She crawls off the stage and sashays over to our table, coming to stand right in front of us.

"What's your name, sweetheart?"

Raven leans into the mic and answers.

"How old are you, Raven?"

"Eighteen."

"Well, on behalf of myself and every queen in this place, we'd like to wish you a very happy birthday."

"Thank you."

Marilyn emerges from behind the bar and casually passes Coco a sparkling tiara.

"Tell me, Raven, how would you like to be an honorary queen for a night?"

Raven lights up and nods her approval. Coco delicately places the crown on top of Raven's head, takes her by the hand, and leads her up to the stage. Tori and Mia shout encouragements from their seats.

"Now, if you wanna be a queen for a night, you're gonna have to own the stage. Do you think you can do that?"

Raven motions for the mic. Coco hands it off.

"Can someone give me a beat?"

The crowd cheers, luring the inner diva we all know and love to come out and play. The DJ selects "Bad Romance" by Lady Gaga. Raven begins to sway her hips sensually, teasingly. I perk up and give her my full, undivided attention. This earns a sharp glance from Emilio. Aside from that, this might not turn out to be such a bad night, after all.

About halfway through the number, an ensemble of drag queens join her onstage. She looks so happy and carefree. I was worried we wouldn't be able to salvage her mood, but based on what I'm seeing, nothing remedies a bruised ego faster than being the center of attention.

Her eyes lock onto mine from across the club. She continues to dance as if I'm the only one watching, single-handedly torturing me with a wicked gleam in her eyes. What's happening right now? Why does she have so much power over me? If only I had that same hold over her.

Suddenly, inspiration strikes in the truest form. I know exactly what I'm going to do to give her that feeling. Too bad she'll have to wait until Thursday night to find out. What I have in mind is arguably the greatest idea in the history of great ideas. Move the fuck over, Edison.

I pound the last of my drink, feeling a renewed sense of confidence. Here's to hanging with cool people, taking big risks, and obliterating comfort zones.

SIX

r a v e n

"Tori, where are my sunglasses?" I yell through the wall.

The sound of squeaking bedsprings resonates, followed by a loud thud.

"Ah, fuck! That hurt."

I shake my head and chuckle. Padded footsteps travel across the hall. Two seconds later, my door swings open to reveal a half-asleep Tori, clad in sweats and a sports bra, massaging the side of her head with an irritated expression on her face. "Come again?"

"Were you napping?"

"Yeah. Kickboxing wore me out."

"Sorry, I didn't mean to wake you."

She yawns and stretches, waging a war with grogginess that will no doubt become second nature once college hits. I can already see the late-night study sessions on the horizon. Might as well introduce coffee and Adderall to my diet now.

"It's all good. What's up?"

"I need my sunglasses."

"Would you believe me if I told you I had no idea where those were?"

I stop applying mascara and glance at her through the mirror. "Not for a second. And if you did lose them, you're dead. Those weren't cheap."

She wanders back into her room to grab them. "What are you getting all dolled up for, anyway?" she hollers.

"I'm going over to Eric's."

"Oh, right. It's Thursday. How was your shift?"

I screw the lid back on the tube and double-check my eyes to make sure they look even. "Insane. We were on an hour-long wait most of the night. I'm surprised I got out of there as early as I did."

Ever since my birthday last week, I've been picking up extra shifts at the restaurant to replenish my pitiful excuse for a savings account. Apparently, time isn't the only thing that flies when you're having fun. Money goes just as fast.

When I initially told my parents I was moving out, they offered to pay my portion of first month's rent as a birthday gift to help ease the transition. I took them up on it. That's how I knew I'd officially reached adulthood. Bills trumped presents. The days of scoring fabulous shoes and accessories are virtually over. I'm on my own now. College tuition is the last remaining link keeping me from somersaulting headfirst into this scary thing known as independence. Failure and poverty are imminent threats.

Tori struts back in and hands me my sunglasses. "Here ya go."

I slip them on top of my head. "Thanks."

"You know, you're putting an awful lot of effort into tonight's appearance. More so than usual, which is saying something."

"Your point?"

"Just making an observation."

I lock eyes with her in the mirror and bring my index finger up to my lips. "Shh."

She grins and nudges me from behind. "Busted."

I spin around to face her. "Verdict?"

She takes a step back and examines the whole outfit from head to toe. I'm rockin' a gray, V-neck, vintage tee with a black blazer, a pair of boyfriend jeans, and black Steve Madden suede pumps. It's the perfect blend of dressy cas, without looking like I tried too hard. Eric will love it.

"Slayin'. Very California girl."

"My thoughts exactly."

I fluff my hair one last time, letting the loose curls cascade down my back, then secure my favorite Audrey Hepburn pendant around my neck. It's a still photograph from *Breakfast at Tiffany's* that my mom gave me for Christmas one year. Grabbing my clutch and keys off my dresser, I make a dash for the hall. Tori follows me out.

"Twenty bucks says you won't be back tonight."

"Oh, whatever."

"Y'all are going to happen. It's inevitable at this point. If you'd pull your heads out of your asses and admit how you really feel about each other, then we could all move on already."

I wink over my shoulder, then close the front door behind me.

I tiptoe over the grass, being extra careful not to dig my heels into the ground. Instead of using the front door like I always do, I head straight for the back. I make a leap for the less-than-impressive slab of concrete Eric insists on calling a patio. Believe me, it's not a patio.

I adjust my shirt and peer inside his windows like a bona fide stalker. His eyes are glued to the TV screen, enraptured by his Xbox game.

Shocker.

I press my torso up against the door. He does a double take and pauses the game. I take it a step further by smushing my nose up against the glass and making a pig face.

He sets the controller down and comes to stand directly in front of me. His gaze drops to my cleavage, then travels back up to my pig face. He leans forward and uses his breath to fog up the glass and writes a message.

I lean back to read the word *sexy* spelled out backwards.

"It's backwards, you idiot."

"No, it's not, dumbass," he says, his voice muffled by the glass.

"Let me in."

"Say pretty please."

"No way."

I seize the handle, but he locks the deadbolt before I get a chance to turn it.

"Eric Matthew Hansen, open this door right now."

He laughs. "Or what? You'll take away TV for a week?"

I rattle the door and search my brain: What do I have the power to take away? There's gotta be something he loves. Clarity strikes. "I'll refuse to make you homemade lasagna for a year."

His smile disappears. "You're bluffing."

"Try me."

His eyes dart back and forth between the doorknob and me. Reluctantly, he succumbs and unlocks the deadbolt. He drags his feet over to the couch and free falls backwards into the cushions. "That threat was uncalled for."

I squeeze inside, shut the door, and carefully remove my heels. "Desperate times call for desperate measures."

He saves his game and turns off the console. I toss my clutch, keys, and sunglasses on his coffee table and head straight to the fridge for a drink.

"Stocked up on snacks."

"Which is why I stick around," I retort.

I steal a tall glass from one of the cupboards and fill it up with Gatorade. I down the first half and let out a satisfying moan, because I was parched, but it comes off erotic. That sound is all it takes to set the tone. Eric's intense gaze falls on me. I pretend to ignore it by staring down at my beverage. It's awfully quiet in here. Why is it so silent? I'm pretty sure he'd be able to hear my stomach gurgle all the way from the couch. I swallow thickly and raise the glass back to my lips, eager to drink my way out of the sexual tension. If this glass doesn't do the trick, I'll just pour another. And another. And another. Until there's no more Gatorade left. *Shit.* Then what am I supposed to do?

Why are things weird between us? Is it because I broke up with Brandon last week? Is it because I'm eighteen? Is it because we're all alone? We've been alone a bazillion times before, but it's never felt so...acknowledged? Maybe it's because for the first time in four years, we're both open to blurring the lines. No more pretenses. No more hiding. No more friend zone. A scenario I've fantasized about since freshman year. So why am I such a nervous wreck? And why is he still looking at me like that? It's distracting.

I tap my nails against the counter and purse my lips. "What movie did you say we're watching again?"

"We aren't watching a movie."

My surprised eyes flick to his. "We aren't?"

"Nope. I owe you a belated birthday present."

My nerves dissipate. "Oh, my God! Where is it? Show me the package. Size is important. I don't care what the other girls say."

He closes the distance between us and takes my hand. "Follow me."

He leads me to the bedroom. I'm intrigued, to say the least. Eric's not one to get overly excited about anything, so this must be good.

In the twelve steps it takes to go from the kitchen to his bedroom, my heart rate has doubled. He reaches over to flip the lights on. A warm glow casts over the room. A plastic tarp is spread out on the floor, protecting the carpet. There's an easel with a blank canvas staged in the center of the room. I haven't seen him whip out one of those since we were neighbors. We've upgraded to painting walls since then. I'm sure you can imagine how ecstatic his landlords get. To his credit, he always paints them back to white before he switches places.

"What's up with the canvas? Are we kickin' it old school?"

"Not exactly."

My brows furrow in confusion.

He rubs the back of his neck sheepishly and pins me with his stare. "I want to paint a portrait of you."

Best. Present. Ever. "I'd be honored, Eric."

"There's something else," he says cautiously, studying my reaction. "Promise me you'll keep an open mind."

My breathing slows. "Why? What do you have in mind?"

"You. Topless."

I blink a few times, processing his request.

"You don't have to if you don't want to," he assures. "But if you're into the idea, I'll make sure everything's covered. I have a certain pose that'll prevent anyone from seeing anything on the painting."

Sounds *Titanic*-esque.

"What's the pose?"

"You'd be standing with your back toward me, looking over your shoulder. Only your back would be exposed."

I'd be way more exposed than that, but I don't bother to correct him. Am I comfortable with being partially nude? In front of him? He's never seen that much of me. No one has. Well, that's not true. Even though I've never experienced a home run, all my other bases have been rounded...just not by Eric.

"You've put a lot of thought into this."

His face goes serious. "You have no idea."

I bite my bottom lip and glance around the room. My eyes settle on the window. I nod in its direction. "Will that be open?"

"I'll need to keep it open to air out the fumes, but the blinds will be closed."

Before I can list all the reasons why I shouldn't do this, the more daring side of me pipes up. "All right, I'm down. But I have a couple stipulations."

"Name them."

"The blinds stay closed, and your mouth stays shut. No exceptions. If I'm gonna do this, I can't have you making side comments and psyching me out."

He slips his hands into his front pockets and rocks back and forth on his heels, struggling to contain his energy. "Deal. I'll grab the brushes and paint while you get situated. If you need to use the bathroom, now's the time to do it. I'm using spray paint and acrylics. The acrylics dry really fast, which means no breaks. Holler when you're ready."

He turns and exits the room, leaving me with some much-needed privacy and a ton of information to digest. I crack the window open and draw the blinds. Incessant pacing and nervous knuckle popping help kill the time. I can't seem to make myself stop. What if I look better with clothes on? I don't want him to be disappointed by what he sees. Sometimes what's left to the imagination is better than what's presented in reality. *Please, God, let me look good naked.*

I conjure every last shred of boldness and shrug off my blazer, letting it fall to the floor with a *whoosh.* I yank off my tee and unhook my bra, adding them to the pile. *Deep breaths,* I remind myself. I look down at my bare feet and wiggle my toes. My eyes scan the room for a mirror. Much to my dismay, there isn't one. I flip my hair over my shoulder and take my place in front of the easel. A light knock on the door catches me by surprise.

"You ready?" Eric checks.

So much for waiting on a cue.

My eyes flutter closed. "Yeah?" It comes out more as a question than an answer.

I mentally kick myself for my lack of confidence.

The door creaks open. He sucks in a sharp breath, making me all too aware of my current state. I swallow hard and open my eyes, keeping them fixated on the wall in front of me. Rustling noises commence. After what seems like an eternity, he speaks.

"Look over your right shoulder, Rave."

I follow directions without giving an ounce of sass. I'm not sure whether I should feel proud or disappointed by this unusual turn of events.

He emerges from behind the easel.

"Don't panic. I'm just going to make a few minor changes. I won't peek, I swear."

He tilts my chin a little further down and fixes my hair. His warm hands caress my shoulders. A rush of chills breaks out over my skin and I tense up.

"Relax, Rave."

"I can't. I feel like I'm being put on display."

"That's because you *are* on display."

"You're not helping."

"I thought you liked having all eyes on you," he gently prods.

"Yeah, but there's a time and place for it."

"Would some music help?"

"Immensely."

"Okay. Don't move." He turns on the stereo and plugs in his iPod. "Any requests?"

"Do you have anything by Prince?"

He actually has the audacity to laugh.

"You belong in a different decade. Nobody listens to Prince anymore."

"Prince is an icon."

"Prince is a has-been."

I roll my eyes. "You're deranged."

"How about some Bon Iver?"

His band choice trumps mine. I nod my approval.

"Which song?"

I pick "Holocene." He hits play and lowers the volume to set the mood.

"Better?"

"Much. Do I look okay? For the portrait, I mean."

His gaze softens. "You're a masterpiece."

That remark effectively shuts me up. It's beyond cheesy, but it's heartfelt.

He moves back around to the easel and picks up a graphite pencil. "Stand as still as possible. This will take a while," he warns.

"'Kay."

"And keep your eyes downcast."

"I thought you wanted them on you."

"Changed my mind."

Who am I to argue with the artist?

As the minutes tick by, I grow more and more relaxed. Watching him in his element, even if it is out of the corner of my eye, is a major turn-on. The sketching goes on for an hour before he switches techniques. When the first glob of paint hits the canvas, I soak up the peaceful sound of the brush strokes. The fumes are great, too. Anytime I go someplace new and register the familiar scent, I always picture Eric. Painting—art in general—will forever be associated with him.

Even though I'm topless, it's nice to know I'm not the only one baring myself. He's putting himself out there, too, only in a different way.

SEVEN

e r i c

She is utter perfection. There's no better way to describe it. And her imperfections are what make her that way. Her courage never ceases to amaze me. Just when I think I've got her figured out, she throws a curveball and knocks me off my game. Like her willingness to go topless—never saw that one coming. Despite her attitude and wardrobe sometimes suggesting otherwise, she's pretty reserved. It's part of the reason I was so uncomfortable asking in the first place.

I don't know why I'm the only person she'll take these risks with, but I'm glad she does. I've seen it time and time again; the stifled good girls are the ones dying to be set free. My guess is it's because rules and boundaries hinder experiences, and Raven had an abundance of them growing up. With me came a whole 'nother world she hadn't been exposed to, and vice versa. We naturally adhere to each other. Like paint to a canvas.

"What are you thinking about?" she asks softly.

It's the first time she's spoken a word in over an hour. We're two hours into the painting session and she's starting to get antsy. To tell you the truth, I'm astonished she's lasted this long. Patience is not her strong suit. I'm pleased with how well the portrait is coming along. The biggest obstacle is capturing her spirit. I want to do her justice.

"You."

A series of emotions dance across her profile, but none of them provoke her to dig for more information.

"What are *you* thinking about?"

"How excited I am to see this painting."

I keep my eyes trained on the canvas to mask how I'm feeling. "I hope you like it."

"I know I will."

Her confidence eases my trepidation.

"I must say, you look—"

She cuts me off with a loud din.

"What?"

"I told you no side comments. Zip it."

"I like you bossy."

She blushes and looks down, shifting back and forth on her feet uncomfortably.

"Stand still," I remind her.

"I'm trying. How much longer do we have? I'm starving. And I have to pee."

"Not long. You're almost done, I promise."

"What about you?"

"I'll need to put the finishing touches on everything before I hand it off. Should be ready in a few days."

"You're giving me the portrait?"

"Duh. It's your birthday gift."

"I thought the experience of you painting me was supposed to be my gift."

"Nope, that's an added bonus," I wink.

She clears her throat. "Have you ever done this before? Painted other women without their clothes on?"

"Yes," I answer truthfully. "But none of them made me feel as nervous as you do. Watching you...it's distracting."

That's an understatement. I feel like a Parkinson's patient. Trembling hands aren't conducive for painting. Deep down, we've always known how we felt about each other, but it rarely gets voiced, especially by her. That is, until she whispers....

"I know the feeling."

Those four words hang in the air, filling up the vacant space inside me. When my heart and hands can't take the tremors anymore, I turn off the stereo and decide to call it a night for the painting portion. I snatch her bra and top up off the floor and move to stand directly behind her. My chest is a breath away from brushing up against her bare back. She stiffens and uses her arms to shield herself protectively.

"Here you go."

She maneuvers around to grab them both out of my hand. "Thanks."

I should leave. Really, I should. But I can't. Not until she tells me to. I reach up and use my hand to sweep her hair over one shoulder, exposing her neck and upper back. Without thinking, I bend down and drop a single kiss between her shoulder blades. Her body shivers.

She turns her head just a fraction and parts her lips. "Eric…" she whispers as a plea.

I don't know if that means "stop" or "never stop," so I follow my instincts.

My fingers lightly trace the contours of her back, igniting a forbidden trail of lust and desire. Her warm skin feels like satin beneath my touch. She lets her head fall back against my shoulder. Her eyelids flutter closed. I lean in and press my lips to her neck. She moans her appreciation. My arms wrap around her torso and pull her flush against me. I want her to feel what she's doing to me.

"Drop your arms, baby," I coax.

Her breathing becomes shallow. She releases her bra and shirt, then winds her arms around the back of my neck, revealing a gorgeous set of curves. My hands grip her waist and slowly glide up her stomach, all the way to her chest. I grab two handfuls and squeeze, then spin her around to face me. Her heated gaze locks onto mine.

"Eric, what are we doing?"

"I have no idea," I confess. "I'm just doing what feels right. Go with it."

For once in my life, I must've said the right thing. She grabs my face and crushes my lips to hers possessively. Raw passion and years of pent-up sexual tension pour free. My fingers tangle in her hair, holding her to me as if she could be ripped away by a tide. Kissing her is the most natural thing in the world. The emotional release feels like we're coming up for air. I've been suffocating for far too long. Begs the question: Why haven't we been doing this all along?

Her fingers seize the hem of my shirt and tug upwards. I take a step back and help her out, then swiftly bring her lips back to mine. Her naked chest feels so good pressed against mine. My legs move toward the bed, taking her with me. I'm extra careful not to stumble into the easel. My heart's beating a million miles a minute, and my thoughts are racing at a similar pace. When my calves reach the edge of the mattress, I fall backwards. She collapses on top of me, her hair fanning our faces. I roll us over and scooch us up while showering her with sporadic kisses.

Before I can take this any further, she hits the brakes.

"Wait a second," she pants, pushing against my chest. I stop my advances and stare at her face. "There's something you should know. I've never done this before."

I push off her body, keeping my weight suspended. "What do you mean?"

She avoids my gaze.

Suddenly, it all becomes clear. "You're a virgin?"

She nods.

I've never been with a virgin. Talk about dropping a bombshell. I make a real effort not to let the concern show on my face. Can I handle this? Can I go there and cross that line? There's no turning back if I do. Am I prepared for what that entails? If I'm being honest with myself, the answer is unclear. What about Raven? Is she ready?

I can't even begin to tell you how badly I want to be her first. The mere thought alone coaxes the territorial, chest-puffing Neanderthal in me to oblige. It's not all about the conquest, though. Far from it.

I cup her chin and force her to meet my gaze. "Then we'll take it nice and slow. Deal?"

She studies me with apprehensive eyes. "I'm worried that I'm not going to be as good as the other girls you've slept with. I've never made it past third base. I don't even know what I'm supposed to do. I mean, I *know* what I'm supposed to do, but I have no idea what the hell I'm doing. Does that make any sense?"

Her vulnerability is disarming. Just when I thought I knew everything. "Rave, I've wanted you for years. *Years.* And now my greatest fantasies are becoming my reality. The anticipation alone is going to do me in, if you know what I'm sayin'. You've got nothing to worry about."

"I don't want to be just another girl—not with you."

"You aren't," I assure. "You're my girl."

She threads her fingers through my hair and gently pulls me back down to her lips. I drop my weight and mold her into the mattress. We're a mess of tangled limbs and jittery emotions, rushed kisses and reverent touches. She's anxious to take this further, and I'm terrified she'll stop.

With shaky hands, she reaches down to unbutton my jeans. Her eyes flicker to mine. I nod, silently urging her to continue. She tugs the zipper and wrestles them down as far as she can. Chuckling, I push myself off the mattress and kick them to the floor. Who needs pants, anyway? I think Thursday Movie Night should include a new pants-free policy for both of us. I'm enforcing this right now. I crouch down and slide hers off until we're both left in our underwear.

Glorious.

I love this new policy.

I fish out a condom from the top drawer of my dresser and dive back onto the bed.

"C'mere," I order, rolling her on top so she's straddling me. I sit up and wind a lock of her hair around my finger and kiss a path from her collarbone to her chest. When my mouth meets her nipple, she gasps.

"How do you wanna do this? Do you want me on top?" I murmur against her skin.

"Yes. Please. Whatever. Anything," she says breathlessly.

"So that's a no, then?"

Leave it to me to throw in a stupid comment.

She rolls her eyes. "You talk too much."

I laugh. My relief couldn't come at a better time. We can't both be a bundle of nerves or this will be a lot less memorable for her than I want it to be.

"My bad," I force her to lie back on the mattress. "Feel free to shut me up."

I don't have to ask twice.

I grab two fistfuls of her underwear and leisurely pull them down her legs, breaking the kiss to toss them over my shoulder. Calmly, I place her hands on the waistband of my boxers.

"Your turn."

Her fingers slip inside and gently tug, revealing all of me. I kick them to the floor and take a deep breath. Humidity and paint fumes pollute the air. Second to Raven's cooking, it's my favorite scent. Our fingers interlace, making this a thousand times more personal. Hand holding before sex? This foreign concept is blowing my mind.

The gesture puts her at ease. It's nice to see her confidence returning. I lift her hands above her head and trap them, then lean forward to recapture her mouth. The gradual build is tantalizing. The slower I kiss her, the faster she breathes. I squeeze her hands in response. With her chest brushing up against mine, all I can focus on is feeling every inch of her body moving fluidly against mine.

When she's ready, I rip open the wrapper and slide the condom on, pumping myself a few times. I lean down and tuck a loose strand of hair behind her ear.

"You sure about this?" I ask, checking for any trace of self-doubt.

"Absolutely."

I drop my head and exhale my relief, then shift my weight accordingly. "Spread your legs."

She complies.

"Grab my torso and take a deep breath."

Her hands grip my sides. She inhales. When the first breath of air slips from her lungs, I sink inside, causing her entire body to tense. I freeze. The sheer pain in her eyes slices me to the core.

"You okay?"

Her jaw clenches. "No. God that hurts."

"Do you want me to stop?"

Honestly, that would be the most disappointing thing to happen in a long time, but I have to ask. I want this to go right for her—for us. I'll do whatever it takes to make that happen.

She shakes her head. "Just go slow and let me get used to it."

I nod and carefully ease further in. She winces. Her fingernails dig deeper into my skin. Inflicting pain on her is self-mutilating. I've never had something feel this right and this wrong all at once. I run my nose along her jawline and try to distract her with kisses.

Gently, I rock my hips into hers, giving her all of me. She wraps her arms around my neck for comfort. I rest my forehead against hers, watching the pain in her eyes gradually fade away and restore with desire.

Once her body fully adjusts, she reciprocates, establishing a rhythm. It's surreal and overwhelming. Soon I forget about everything and concentrate on chasing the pleasure.

"Better?"

She nods and rakes her fingers through my hair. "Don't stop."

Not planning on it. A sheen of sweat covers my skin as my body continues to worship hers. Each time I move, I lose another piece of myself in her. I don't care. She can have all my pieces. She's the only person who I could lose everything to and still manage to feel whole.

"You feel extraordinary."

She groans.

My head drops to watch our hips meet. I'm connected to her in every way and it's still not close enough. What the hell have I been missing? Tingles burst in the base of my spine and heighten the experience. Before I get a chance to warn her, I'm shuddering into bliss. Once I catch my breath, I pull out and reach down, continuing to pleasure her with my hands. She wraps her legs around my torso, arches her back, and follows me there.

When we're both sated, I drop and roll over to stare at the ceiling, basking in the temporary high. The silence is comforting. The void inside me is subdued, at least for now.

I get up to remove the condom and rejoin her on the bed. Without the slightest hesitation, I reach for her hand. I'd never be this open with anyone else. She twists her head, a huge grin sweeping across her face.

"What?" I smile, still staring at the ceiling.

"Nothing."

I squeeze her hand affectionately. "Tell me."

She curls into my side and rests her head on my chest. Her fingers lightly stroke my abdomen. "I can't believe that just happened."

I kiss the crown of her head. "How are you feeling?"

"Sore but good at the same time."

"There's Advil in the bathroom if you need it. Help yourself."

She's too lost in thought to answer.

"What's up?"

"Just thinking."

"Sounds exhausting. You know what else is exhausting? Mind reading."

She pinches me.

"Ouch." I flip over onto my side and scoot down so we're eye level. "Fine, I'll play along. What are you thinking about?"

She caresses my temple. Her hand floats down to my cheek, tracing small circles with her thumb. "Why don't you ever talk about your past?"

My face falls. The state of euphoria I'm currently in vanishes. *What the fuck?* Is she really going to broach that subject after what just transpired between us? I swallow the rising panic and attempt to brush it off.

"Because it's boring and there's nothing to tell. Why are you bringing this up all of a sudden?"

She shrugs nonchalantly like it's a simple, harmless topic. "Because it's the one area of your life that I know so little about."

"Barring my old therapist, you know more than anyone."

"But it's still not much. It's surface details like your dad running off and your mom losing custody. You've never told me why those things happened."

"And it's going to stay that way."

She stops stroking my face. "You don't have any intention of telling me? Ever?"

"Why would I?"

She quickly disentangles from our embrace and props herself up on an elbow to stare down at me. Her face is a mixture of confusion and hurt. "Why wouldn't you? I tell you everything. Do you not trust me enough to let me in?"

"It's not that," I reassure. "I just don't see the point. It doesn't serve any purpose. The past is in the past. It's been dealt with a long time ago. I have no desire to rehash any of that shit and run the risk of tainting what we have."

I raise my hand to brush her cheek with the backs of my knuckles, but she swerves out of the way. She pulls the bed sheet up to shield herself.

"Eric, it does serve a purpose. Your past is part of who you are. It doesn't define you, but it shapes you. I'm not saying you need to divulge everything right here and now, but you can't seriously expect me to be in a one-sided relationship. That's not fair. If we're giving this a real shot, and I'm putting myself out there, then I expect the same in return. Do you really think that's too much to ask for?"

I can't even tell you what she said during that last bit because I got hung on the word—"Who the hell said anything about a relationship?"

She rears back as if I've slapped her. I watch the various emotions play out across her face. Everything from shock to devastation surfaces. Her grip on the sheet tightens as she crawls off the bed. I immediately sit up and go into repair mode.

"Rave, that's not how I meant it."

No response.

Shit. What have I done?

She darts around the floor and gathers her clothes in one hand, avoiding my gaze at all costs. I run my hands through my hair, frantically searching for a way to explain myself. It's not that I don't want her to be my girlfriend, but it was never discussed. The statement caught me off guard. I should've figured that's what she wanted, but she's shot me down so many times before I've gotten in the habit of no longer making assumptions.

"Rave, listen to me."

She shakes her head and moves to the door.

"Where are you going?"

"Home."

"Wait!" I jump off the bed and wrap my fingers around her arm to stop her. She looks down at my hand, then up at me. Her beautiful brown eyes are searing with fury.

"Let go," she snaps.

I try for pleading. "Stay the night and we can sort this out."

"After that? Not a chance."

She rips her arm free and opens the door. I slip into my boxers and flinch when the door slams behind her. I throw on my tee and race out there before she can reach the bathroom. She beats me by three lousy steps and locks me out.

I raise my fist and bang on the door. "Rave, open up. We need to talk."

She rebuttals with a proposition of her own. "Go fuck yourself!"

I press my head against the door and lower my voice. "I didn't know, okay? I didn't know that's what you wanted."

I hear faint scattered sounds, then her voice echoes from the other side of the door. "Oh, really? So you just decided to skip over the part where I specifically told you I didn't want to be like every other girl?"

"Do you honestly think if you were like any other girl we'd even be having this conversation? Shouldn't that tell you something?"

"It tells me I was right all along. You can't handle real commitment. Instead, you choose to shut me out. You love to joke how I'm the selfish one, but really it's you. You're completely incapable of putting anyone else's needs above your own. You only care about casual, meaningless sex. It's all a stupid game that allows you to get what you want from others, without having to compromise anything yourself. At least I'm not afraid to put myself out there and let somebody see me for who I really am. But you, you're so busy running from your past and dodging intimacy, you wouldn't know affection if it hit you in the balls with a two-by-four."

The door flies open, making me jump back. She zips her jeans up and plows past me with her salty attitude and thoroughly fucked hair.

I trail her into the living room. "Will you slow down for two seconds? I'm trying to fix the problem, but you're not letting me."

"Don't bother."

"Now who's shutting who out?"

She snatches her keys and clutch up, slides her sunglasses on top of her head, and holds onto the wall while she wrestles into her heels. "Don't go there. Don't you dare put this on me. I laid everything out on the table and told you exactly what I wanted, exactly what I was afraid of, and exactly what my issue is."

"But you *didn't* tell me exactly what you wanted. That's my point! You never said you wanted a relationship."

"Do you really think I would've slept with you otherwise? Use your other head for once."

I let out a defeated sigh, realizing I can't win in this scenario. "You know what? Fine. Be that way. You wanna walk out that door, go right ahead. I can't stop you. But you could at least tell me how to make it better."

She opens the patio door and shoots one last lethal glance over her shoulder. "Figure it out yourself."

There goes the second door slam of the night, and the millionth door slam of my lifetime. All that's left is me standing in an empty apartment harboring two distinct feelings I'm all too familiar with: guilt and self-loathing.

EIGHT

r a v e n

Three days have passed and still no word from Eric. To add insult to injury, every time I creep on his Facebook or Instagram, new pictures emerge of him flaunting his "no strings attached" lifestyle. Just this morning there was a photo posted of him and some random brunette getting close at a bar last night. It's like he's deliberately rubbing it in my face to make me jealous. He's not doing anything out of the ordinary from what he usually does on social media, but now it hurts. You'd think he'd have the decency to spare me the trashy photos. Or maybe he took my feelings into consideration and did it anyway. A dull ache spreads through my chest at the thought.

Had I known our night was going to end with a blowup fight, I would've never let him have me. It all happened so fast. One minute everything was perfect, and the next it all spun out of control. My heart feels as raw and used as my body. It wasn't until I was getting ready this morning and looking in the mirror that I was forced to face the ugly truth: I got played.

What was I expecting? Have I really become one of *those* girls? The typical, cliché ones who fall into the embarrassing trap of believing they're the exception and not the norm? I was thoroughly convinced Eric and I had something different. I've never felt more stupid. Did he really think I'd settle for being his sidepiece? That I wouldn't want a relationship? It was supposed to be obvious. Apparently, Eric needs it spelled it out in bold letters, underlined three times, highlighted, and stapled to his forehead.

"Raven, clock out and go home."

I glance over at Andre. "Why? My shift doesn't end for another forty-five minutes."

"I know, but we're slow and I can't use you."

Normally I'd be all over getting cut early, but I was really counting on the distraction today.

"Are you sure?"

"Positive. If we get slammed tonight, I'll call you back in."

There's that conflict of interest again.

"Sounds good. See ya later."

I remove my apron, grab my stuff from the back, and clock out. Digging through my purse, I find my phone and check for any missed notifications. A few texts pop up on the screen. Much to my disappointment, none of them are from Eric. How much longer is this standoff going to last? Better yet, who's going to be the first to surrender?

Tori: *When are you off? I'm bored out of my mind.*

Tori: *Come watch Grey's with me. Oh, and bring home some stuffed mushrooms and mozzarella sticks if you can, purdy please. I'm too lazy to shower and drive there myself. Don't judge.*

I smile and shake my head when I finish reading those texts.

Me: *You're becoming completely unmanageable.*

It only takes her a few seconds to respond.

Tori: *I know, but you love me. ;)*

Me: *Just clocked out. I'll put the order in and head out. Be there soon(ish).*

Tori: *You're my hero. XOXO.*

Me: *Lies.*

Tori: *Truth.*

When I walk through the door, I find Tori sprawled out on the couch in her pajamas, scrolling through Instagram. She tilts her head back to greet me, kicks her feet up on the coffee table, and points to the cushion beside her. I pass the appetizers off and tell her to hold on a sec while I grab a couple forks from the kitchen.

"Have you seen Eric's posts today?"

I bump the drawer closed with my stomach and spin around to retrieve a bottle of wine from the fridge. I'm not revisiting this topic sober. It's less painful to process when the details are blurry and self-awareness takes an extended vacation. I fetch two wine glasses from the top cupboard and fill them to the brim with Merlot. I shove the cork back in the bottle, sling it under my arm, and walk over to take a seat, carefully handing her a glass.

"Not since this morning. Why?"

She takes a sip and sets her glass down to show me her screen. I look closely at the most recent photo. It's a selfie of Eric and me taken two years ago when we were hanging out in an empty movie theater. My head is casually resting against his shoulder without a care in the world. We're both sporting 3D glasses. Our cheeks are puffed out to the max, I'm cross-eyed, and he's staring longingly at my bucket of popcorn. The caption underneath the photo reads: *My best friend for life. #homegirl #rideordie #throwback*

I remember that day perfectly. Having the theater to ourselves was awesome. We spent the entire movie talking about random stuff and messed around with the projector, making inappropriate hand gestures on the screen. We loaded up on snacks like it was going out of style, then we each stood on opposite ends of the aisle and took turns tossing gummy bears in the air for the other one to catch in their mouth. To this day, neither of us could tell you what the movie was about.

Tori's voice knocks me out of my nostalgia. "You think it's his way of trying to apologize?"

I hand the phone back and gulp a generous amount of wine before responding. "If it is, I'm not impressed. He needs to step it up and try something sincere. Reaching out via social media is impersonal and overdone, especially when he's been posting countless photos of him with *other* girls all weekend long. He should know me better than that. And if he doesn't, he has no business posting that photo in the first place."

"Has he tried texting you at all since Thursday?"

"Nope," I emphasize the "p" with a popping sound.

"Have you tried getting ahold of him?"

I shake my head. "And I don't plan on it, either."

"Atta girl. Make him work for it."

"More like make him suffer. These last few days have been hell. If he were feeling even a fraction of what I am, he'd be speed dialing me nonstop and blowing up my phone with text messages. And if he couldn't get ahold of me that way, he'd race over here to break down my door and beg me to give him a second chance. He's doing neither of those things. He'd rather be out in bars picking up random chicks instead of trying to make it right with the one girl who's never left his side. How insulting is that? I put myself out there in the greatest way possible and he made me feel so insignificant. A small part of me hates him."

"Hey," Tori soothes, wrapping her arms around my torso and giving me a tight hug. "You don't mean that. You're just upset. Rightfully so, but still."

Tears well up in my eyes. "How could he do this to me? I trusted him. And the way he made me feel about myself afterwards? That's the worst part. I had to pull my car over because I was crying so hard I thought I was going to puke. He ruined everything."

"If it makes you feel any better, my first time was awful. Nick didn't even try to comfort me. Or get me off. My body was sore for days and the whole experience was so traumatizing, I didn't have sex again for a year. Remember that? Felt like the world's longest dry spell, but I couldn't bring myself to do it."

She repositions her legs on the couch. "I know it's probably too soon to tell, but do you think y'all will be able to move past this and salvage the friendship? I mean, you've been friends for a really long time. That's a lot of great memories to throw away. On the other hand, he royally fucked up. We can't ignore that. Maybe he should be exiled. Decisions, decisions."

I stare down and pick an invisible piece of lint off my work pants. "I don't know. I have no idea where we go from here. All I know is I'm exhausted. Let's drop the conversation for now. I'd like to give my mind a break from all the obsessing and have a fun girls night. Let's stuff ourselves with bomb ass food, drown our sorrows in wine, and overdose on McDreamy."

Tori raises her hand high in the air. "Preach! But first, let's have a Kodak moment."

She picks up her phone, swipes her screen, and pulls up Instagram. She holds the camera out in front of us. Before she snaps the picture, she drops her hand. "Hold up! We need our wine."

Both of us seize our glasses and squeeze back into the picture.

"My eyes are all red and puffy." I complain.

"That's what filters are for."

"Good call."

Cue the fraudulent smile. A momentary flash goes off, followed by the clicking sound. Tori sets her wine back on the table and alters the photo to make us look like goddesses. I start up Netflix and search for the second season of *Grey's Anatomy*. It's the only one I can binge-watch in my current frame of mind. Meredith + Derek = Happiness? I'll pass. Give me the angst and heartache.

I hit play and drop the remote on the couch. Tori leans over to show me the final shot. "Check it out."

Strangely enough, I look happy. Guess the saying holds true: appearances can be deceiving, and artificial smiles can go a long way.

"Post it."

She taps her screen, types a speedy message, and uploads the photo. I steal her phone out of her hand to check out the caption.

Who needs boys when you got bad bitches? Real love never dies. #ourloveisobscene #realtalk #stepoff

I smile—a genuine one this time—and pass the phone back.

"Truth."

We grab our forks and dig in. Food has been missing its usual pizzazz lately, and my appetite is suffering as a result. *How long can a person survive on a diet of red wine?* Probably not long. I should google that.

Answer: it's complicated.

Not promising.

One glass of red wine is good for your heart, though. Too bad I'm on my third. Ugly crying and boy bashing are parked in the forefront of my mind, waiting for me to jump in and take a joy ride. Meanwhile, Meredith's wandering around on my TV screen like a lost puppy, baring her dark and twisty soul, imploring Derek to "Pick me. Choose me. Love me." Spoiler alert: he picks Addison. Ruthless bastard. I feel ya, Mer. We can't win for losing. Pour yourself a glass of wine when you're done with surgery and catch up with me.

My pity party is cut short when my phone buzzes. Eric's face lights up the screen under his designated nickname, Modern Day James Dean.

My heart sinks.

Tori picks up the remote and hits pause. "Who is it?"

"Eric. Should I answer?"

"Only if you're ready to talk."

It's not a question of whether or not I'm ready to talk; it's whether I'm willing to listen to what he has to say. Before I can make a decision, the call ends and travels into my missed calls log. Another missed shot. Story of our lives. Our relationship—or lack thereof—is defined precisely by the number of opportunities we were presented and never took. What's holding us back? Fear of rejection? Fear of failure? Fear of accepting a love that's powerful enough to destroy our safe crutch of dependency? I'm gonna go with all the above.

My phone vibrates with an incoming text.

MDJD: *Look outside your door.*

Is he serious? I stand up and walk over to the front door, pressing my hands up against it and peering through the peephole. There's no one on the other side. I step back and swing it open. A medium-sized canvas wrapped in brown paper tips over and lands on my feet. Curious, I glance around the empty hallway and crouch down to pick it up.

"What's that?" Tori asks.

I drag it in and kick the door shut. "One of Eric's portraits."

She hustles over to my side, "Ooh! Let me see," and rips the paper off.

We both stare.

Speechless.

Streaks of midnight blue paint run up the canvas and fan out like splashes of water on dried paper. Vibrant shades of magenta are infused at the top, elevating the mood from somber to serene. Flocks of ravens soar above my head in a vanilla cream sky, keeping their watchful eyes on me.

At first glance, I appear closed-off and solemn. But if you study the painting more closely, I think I just look…innocent. He captured my essence, not my outside, my inside. A perfect blend of vulnerability and strength. He even scribbled his signature in the bottom right corner, sealing his stamp of approval.

"Wish I had someone to see me the way Eric sees you," Tori mutters in awe.

I cannot stop smiling. Knowing Eric put so much thought and effort into my gift chips away a thin layer of the icy exterior cloaking my heart. If this is his way of reaching out, I accept. We're still not okay, but at least we're moving in the right direction.

I set the canvas against the couch and snap a quick photo. I send it to Eric as an attachment along with the message: *Thank you so much for the portrait. It's gorgeous. I'll send you a pic when it's up on the wall.*

Baby steps.

Several beats pass before he responds.

MDJD: *Can I call you?*

I tap my thumb nail against the screen while I mull that over.

Tori's voice cuts through my indecisiveness. "Just call him, Rave. You know you want to."

She's right, but I don't want to give in too soon. He doesn't deserve to be let off the hook that easily. The only thing worse than being a cliché girl who falls into the trap of believing she's the exception, is one who does it over and over again. Live and learn, raise the bar, and whatever you do, don't settle. That last rule applies to both men and shoes.

I type out a curt response.

Me: *Not tonight.*

Voilà! Bar's been set.

NINE

e r i c

"How much longer is this gonna last?"

Funny, I could ask Mrs. Norman the same thing. Every Tuesday the woman finds something new to bitch about. Never fails. This time she's complaining about how long it's taking me to mow her lawn. I know that sounds sexual, but it's not. She's a tad too old for me. Anyone who requires arthritis medication and a cane for transportation cannot handle Yours Truly. Besides, necrophilia is not my style. Also, I'm actually about to mow her lawn.

I drop the gate on the back of my truck and pull the trimmer out.

"Should be done in about thirty minutes, Mrs. Norman."

"Good. I don't know why it's taking so long. I don't pay you to sunbathe out here. And stop blowing grass onto my sidewalk."

"Yes, ma'am."

"Pull your pants up, too. I don't wanna see that trash when I'm lookin' out my window."

I doubt she can see anything beyond her nose, but I'll save that argument for another Tuesday. It's taken me twice as long to get all my jobs done because I'm down a coworker. I'm on my fourth job site with one more to go. Next comes H-E-B, which will effectively screw me out of the rest of my day. At least I'm almost done here, but not before she adds another jab.

"Come to think of it, you might wanna buy a new pair of pants. Preferably ones that don't have paint stains running down the legs. Learn to look professional, young man."

Please slit my throat with a lawnmower blade. I'm begging you.

I'm sorry, was that too morbid?

Seriously, though. If she keeps it up, I'm tagging her house tonight. A little graffiti will teach her some tolerance. Maybe then she'll learn to appreciate my art.

She takes her wrinkled ass back inside her house, leaving me in peace to trim. I start that bad boy up and go to town, deeply fantasizing about walking into her house and slicing all of her furniture up. Puts a smile on my face and an extra step in my stride.

As I'm loading up the truck and trailer, my phone vibrates in my pocket. I wipe the sweat off my forehead with the back of my arm and check the text.

Levi: *Hey, long time no see. Party at my place tonight. Bring some girls.*

Me: *What are we celebrating?*

Levi: *I'm a free man.*

In other words, he's fresh out of jail. Probably on probation, too. Dumbass. It's been awhile since we've crossed paths. He decided to break off and do his own thing. Moved on to heavier crimes like theft and battery. I'm all for taking risks, but they've gotta be calculated. Levi's reckless. Once I saw him hopping on a first-class train to Nowheresville, I chucked up the deuces and paved my own way instead.

Me: *I'll be there. You cool if I invite Chase Williams?*

Levi: *Only if you each bring a girl to balance it out. This party's not going to be a sausage fest.*

Me: *Fair enough. See you in a bit.*

I scroll through my contacts until I find Chase.

Me: *Party at Levi's place tonight. Bring at least one female.*

Chase: *I'm off at 9. I'll text some girls and swing by after work.*

Me: *Sounds good.*

Next comes Mia.

Me: *My buddy's having a party tonight and he's requesting dirty, low-down hookers. Shall we count you in attendance?*

Mia: *Why would you need me to make an appearance if you're showing up?*

Me: *Ha-ha. If only you were funny. But seriously, is that a no?*

Mia: *I can't tonight. Sorry. My dad and I have plans.*

Me: *Whatever. We're too cool for you anyway.*

Mia: *Now who's the funny one?*

Me: *;)*

Saving the best for last, I pull up Raven's number. I've spent the last few nights reminiscing and rereading all of our previous text messages, dating back as far as they'll go. Every time I'm reminded of what I said, guilt seeps into my conscious and hijacks my brain. How could I have been such an idiot? I had her, dammit! She was right within my grasp and now she's barely speaking to me. I never realized how depressingly hollow everything is when she's not around.

Instead of shooting her a text, I hit the call button and hold the phone up to my ear, waiting for her to answer. That's assuming she will.

To my surprise, she does.

"Hello?"

"Hey…" I stammer, looking down and shuffling my feet.

Great. Now it's awkward and forced. I make a lame attempt to recover. "How are you?"

"Fine."

Liar. No matter how much she tries to deny it, I know she's hurting. I wish I could wrap my arms around her and heal every wound I've caused. No doubt she'd break my hands off if I tried. Any chance I had of winning her over was lost the second I made her feel like she was nothing more than a piece of ass. Mending fences has never seemed so difficult. I don't even know where to begin. If only it were a simple fix. Since laughter is the best remedy…. "A much less attractive version of Betty White just spent the limited breaths she has left chewing me out."

"Good."

Despite the one-word response, I hear her smile on the other end of the line. A tiny fissure in her armor. Progress. "How long are you going to keep busting my balls?"

"Depends."

"On?"

"On when you redeem yourself."

"You can't stay mad at me forever, you know."

Silence.

I check the screen to make sure she didn't hang up on me. Her picture's still showing. *Stay with me, Rave.*

"Give me a chance to make it up to you tonight," I cajole.

"How?"

"Come to Levi's party and I'll explain everything."

"I'm not invited to Levi's party."

"You are now. I'm inviting you."

She laughs bitterly. "Why in the world would I want to go to one of Levi's stupid parties? You know I can't stand him. He's a dick to me every time I see him."

Levi's convinced I'm pussy-whipped and believes Raven is solely responsible for why I never come around anymore. Truth is his ego couldn't handle it when I started hanging out with her on a regular basis. I was sick of taking the heat for his fuckups. I saw an easy out, and I took it.

"Because I'll be there, and I want to see my best friend. I miss you. At least give me a chance to explain myself. That's all I'm asking. I know you're pissed—and you have every right to be—but there's a reason why I reacted the way I did."

It suddenly dawns on me that my relationships are usually comprised of endless "let me explain" moments and genuine misunderstandings. Gets old very quickly.

"Are Tori and Mia going?"

"I texted Mia, but she's busy. Haven't tried Tori yet. Bring her along if you want. Whatever you do, just show up. This is me begging. You know I don't beg."

"I'll think about it," is all she offers.

Frustrated, I run my hand through my hair. "Rave, please?"

I wait patiently on the line while she considers my request. I'd give anything for this one thing to go right today. All I need is for her to show up. The rest I can handle on my own. I'll improvise.

Several beats pass before she finally speaks.

"Fine, I'll go. But I'm only staying for an hour."

Every muscle in my body relaxes. It's not quite as long as I would've hoped for, but at least she agreed.

"Do you want me to pick you up?"

"No, I'll drive myself. That way you can stay and have fun."

What I really want is to leave when she does and spend some alone time with her, but I decide not to press my luck.

"Thank you." And because I can't resist, I make her an offer she won't be able to refuse. "If you're interested, there's a way you can torture me."

"I'm listening."

"Wear one of those skimpy little outfits hidden in your closet."

"Nice try. Sweatpants it is."

I roll my eyes and call her bluff. "You don't even own a pair of sweatpants."

"No, but Tori does. So thanks for the inspiration."

"Well, I'm sure you'll look sexy regardless."

"I'll go to great lengths to ensure I don't."

"No you won't. You care way too much about what other people think. And even if you did, it wouldn't work. You're always beautiful to me."

She sucks in a sharp breath. I jump on the opportunity to have the last word.

"Can't wait to see you tonight."

I end the call and slip my phone back into my pocket, feeling a glimmer of hope for the first time in five days.

I burst through Levi's door and walk straight into a dense cloud of marijuana smoke. The scent triggers a slew of memories to come rushing back. It's been a while since I rolled up a joint and chilled the fuck out. Miss those days. I inhale a deep breath and trudge on.

In true Levi fashion, the place is crammed with chicks, drugs, and an endless supply of booze. There's a crowd mingling around the kitchen table, watching a game of strip poker that's underway. Slices of pizza and cups of jungle juice are lined up for grabs on the counter. Lyrics from 2Pac's "California Love" are pounding through the speakers.

I weave through the masses and search for Levi. He's reclining on the living room couch with a beer in one hand, and a handful of ass in the other. A tattooed, curvy redhead is straddling his lap, whispering sweet nothings in his ear. When he sees me approaching, he nudges her off and stands up.

"Sup, man?" he pulls me into a one-arm hug.

"Not shit."

He releases me and looks down at the bottle I'm holding. A cross between confusion and disgust erupts on his face. "Sangria? Have you grown a vagina since I last saw you?"

"Fuck off. It's for Raven. She likes the sweet stuff."

His face goes serious. "You invited that buzzkill to my party?"

"Relax. She knows how to have a good time."

"Naw, man. She's a priss. Please tell me you brought a backup?"

"She may or may not be bringing a friend."

"You've gotta be kidding me."

"If memory serves, you used to have the hots for her," I remind him.

"Times change. And so do people." He shoots me an accusatory look.

"Come on, she isn't that bad."

"She's a beauty, but she ain't worth it. Her hotness is consumed by the amount of bullshit you have to put up with. I've been telling you that for years."

"Hey, do you hear that? It's a beer calling my name," I say, cutting the conversation short and slapping him on the shoulder. "Glad to see you're a free man."

He takes a sip of his own. "Yeah, yeah, whatever. I'll hit you up later if Queen Buzzkill hasn't gotten to you first."

I roll my eyes. "Let it go, dude."

I dip into the kitchen before he has a chance to respond. Can somebody say mindtrip? It's crazy what time and distance will do to a person. Although, I'm sure he'd say the same about me. Levi was the closest thing I had to a brother. Raven was an outsider who didn't understand our lifestyle. These days, the roles have reversed. Levi's been quietly fading into obscurity as I rely on Raven to hold me down and keep me sane. She's my thread of stability in a world full of uncertainties.

Speaking of my favorite ball buster, in prances Raven—solo. My jaw drops. She definitely took my advice and ditched the sweatpants idea. She's flaunting her generous curves in a fiery red, body-hugging dress, which I'm certain was single-handedly plucked off a hanger in hopes to destroy me. Mission accomplished. The bold, dramatic color suits her personality perfectly.

My body drifts towards her like a magnet to a fridge. When she sees me coming, she stiffens. I hesitate briefly, allowing my eyes roam every inch of her scorching figure. It hurts to look at her. All it does is remind me of what I've known all along—I don't deserve her. I bend down to kiss her temple and slip a compliment in her ear. "Congratulations. I'm eating my heart out."

She twists her head in my direction, revealing a set of cold, calculated eyes. "You should be after you kicked me in mine."

I straighten my spine and stifle a grin. Vengeful banter turns me on.

I raise the bottle of sangria. "Peace offering?"

"Liquoring me up isn't going to help our situation, Eric."

"You sure about that? It can't hurt."

She shakes her head. "Always deflecting with a joke. What a shocker."

My face goes from playful to serious as I prepare to tell her off.

"Hey, I bent over backwards trying to get you to come around. You wouldn't budge. That's on you, not me."

She coils her fists and steps in my lane, going from 0 to 100 real quick. "You tried once. Once! And that was after you were out whoring around in bars and bragging about it on social media the very next day. How do you think that made me feel? What happened between us was a huge deal for me. I put myself out there in every way possible, and you moved on to the next thing without even blinking. It's all part of the fun, right? The game doesn't work if someone doesn't get played, and it had to be me."

I reach over and slam the bottle down on the counter, drawing lots of unwanted attention. "Is that what you think? That this is all a game to me? That I don't have real, genuine feelings for you? That I haven't wanted you from day one? How many times have I pursued you over the years? You don't need to tell me what we have because I've seen it all along. And if you would've waited long enough for me to explain myself instead of storming out of my apartment like some scorned ex-girlfriend with an axe to grind, you'd know how much I wanted to make this work."

"Then why did you freak out when I mentioned a relationship?"

I rake my hands through my hair. "Because the thought scares me, okay? I'm not used to commitment, and I'm afraid of losing you. Imagine my disappointment when it took me less than five minutes to fuck everything up once I finally had you. Do you think that's fair to either of us? Now I'm second-guessing what I'm capable of giving you. I should've read between the lines when you told me you didn't want to be like all the other girls, but I didn't want to assume anything, especially with our history. I was so fixated on the bigger picture that I missed what was happening right in front of me. I'm sorry. I never meant to hurt you or make you feel inadequate. And for the record, I wasn't out in bars picking up chicks. Erase that shit from your mind."

Tons of curious partygoers are watching the scene play out like a bad car accident. Pretty sure some are placing bets on my fate. They're not the only ones hanging on the edge of their seats. I'm anxious to see how this argument ends, too.

She backs up, confused. "What do you mean you're second-guessing what you're capable of giving me?"

Levi casually leans against the fridge, slipping into the conversation like a hot poker ready to brand Raven. "He's saying you aren't worth the hassle." His bloodshot eyes find mine. "Told you she was a buzzkill."

I glare at him. "Shut up."

"Screw you, Levi," Raven snaps.

He motions towards the door with his beer. "Y'all can leave now. I don't need this drama at my party. Thanks to her, there's a new rule in effect: No Cunts Allowed."

Raven's eyes grow wide with shock. The room becomes a blur. Before I can process what's happening, I turn and swing my arm as hard as I can until my fist collides with Levi's face. Sharp pain flares over my knuckles. He stumbles sideways into the poker table, spilling all its contents. Chair legs scrape against the tile, backing away. Half-naked players jump out of their seats, dropping their cards and clearing a path. Something dark and sinister takes root inside of me as I lunge for him.

"Eric! Stop!" Raven cries.

I ignore her plea and channel all my rage into tearing up Levi's face, unleashing years of pent-up resentment and aggression. He returns the favor, getting a few solid hits of his own in and knocking me to the ground. Two girls scream and flee the room.

I grab him by the collar of his tee and bring his face close to mine. "You ever talk about her like that again, I'll break your fuckin' jaw," I threaten.

He laughs deliriously. "You ain't shit. Never have been."

I raise my fist to deliver another crushing blow, but someone puts a stop to the madness and pulls me into a standing position.

"Enough!" Chase steps in front, using his body as a barrier. He puts a hand on my chest and looks over his shoulder at Levi, then back at me. "Reel it in before the cops get called."

My gaze floats to Raven. She's studying me with trepidation. Her chest is rising and falling as rapidly as mine. I catch my breath and glance down at my crimson-stained knuckles. A surge of heat floods my body, making the throbbing intensify. Adrenaline must be wearing off.

Guests trickle back into the kitchen, sharing hushed conversations about me like I'm not here. So fucking awkward. Levi stands and wipes the blood leaking from his nose. He checks his booze and blood-soaked clothes and evaluates the damage. His furious eyes find mine. "Get the fuck out and take your friends with you. We're done here."

Famous last words.

"Come on, let's go," Chase urges.

I reach behind for Raven's hand and pull her into my side. The three of us head for the door. Abruptly, Raven stops and shakes her hand free. She scurries back into the kitchen to grab her sangria off the counter and holds it up in front of Levi. "This is mine, dickhead."

I crack a smile through my split lip, registering the metallic taste of blood. We dash out the door without bothering to look back.

When we reach the parking lot, Chase slows his pace and says, "I can't take you two anywhere, can I?"

"Apparently not," Raven mutters. "Thanks for showing up when you did. You saved Eric from getting arrested."

"Aw, were you worried about me?" I nudge her teasingly.

"Not really. I just don't want you to be immortalized in an orange jumpsuit. Mug shots last forever. The color doesn't suit your complexion."

"I'd be more concerned about him dropping the soap," Chase argues.

I groan. "My face aches. How bad is the damage?"

"Not as bad as Levi's."

"I can't believe you hit him. What were you thinking?" Raven chides.

"You said you wanted to be out of there early. Sacrifices had to be made."

She pushes my shoulders.

"Easy, woman. I'm wounded."

Chase turns his head. "Seriously, though. What happened in there?"

"He called Raven a C U Next Tuesday."

His eyes widen. "What?"

"Yeah," Raven scoffs. "Threw me for a loop."

"What a dick. He deserved every punch."

"Guys, where are we going?" Raven asks.

We all stop and give each other blank stares.

"My place?" I suggest. "There's beer."

"Works for me," Chase says, whipping out his phone. "Let me text these girls I contacted earlier and tell them the party's off."

I look over to gauge Raven's mood. "What about you?"

She shrugs. "Count me in, I guess."

She's down to hang. A promising sign. Does this mean things will go back to normal? Because I firmly believe defending her honor and getting my face bashed in deserves across-the-board forgiveness. Regardless, this is the first time she's going to set foot in my apartment since last Thursday. I'm hoping that won't interrupt the healing process.

If this complicated mess has taught me anything, it's that I'm not willing to risk the friendship a second time. It doesn't change the way I feel about her, but I need her in my life. She's too valuable. If that means I'm the guy she cries to instead of for, then so be it. I'll be the demoted, non-gay bestie with a comfortable shoulder, an ear primed for bitch fits, a freezer stocked with Ben & Jerry's, and round-the-clock blue balls. Serves me right for trying to fix something that wasn't broken in the first place.

TEN

r a v e n

I'm struggling to keep up with all the insanity. Eric torpedoes through life at a ridiculously high speed, racing through every moment like a shooting star in the night sky. Just when you think you've caught a glimpse and zoom in, he's moved on to the next thing. The only traces left behind are his spasmodic paintings. Me? I can't move that fast. My four-inch heels won't allow it. I like to hang back and window-shop my way through life, absorbing all there is to see. Whirlwind events are about as common in my world as a fashion faux pas.

Despite all the chaos, Eric keeps dusting himself off and blasting forward with no real set goal or plan. That fly-by-the-seat-of-your-pants mentality comes in handy for nights like this when it all gets to be too overwhelming. He doesn't even have to stop and think about it. Unfortunately, that's not a quality I possess.

Another quality I don't possess: the ability to sweep things under the rug and pretend like nothing ever happened. Eric may be over our little spat and his blowout fight with Levi, but I'm not. No matter how hard I try to shed the memories, they won't die. Violent images and bittersweet words are permanently seared into my skull.

"Hold still," I tell him.

He winces under the ice pack.

"Shit, that's cold."

"It'll help with the swelling."

"You know what else helps? Having my own personal nurse."

"You hear that, Chase?" I holler. "Eric wants you to dress up and play nurse."

Eric pinches my inner thigh, making me jerk.

Chase emerges from the bathroom and heads for the fridge. "Wouldn't doubt it."

Eric perks up. "Hey, grab me another beer while you're at it, will ya? The alcohol's dulling the pain."

Chase obliges.

Eric pops the cap, tosses his head back, and drains half the bottle. I'm momentarily dazed by the way his throat moves when he drinks, his lips pressed firmly to the rim of the glass. Recollections of how good those lips tasted and felt when they were moving with mine come rushing back.

Stop picturing these things.

Chase sits down next to me on the coffee table and inspects the corners. "Where did you get this thing?"

"Goodwill," Eric answers.

"That explains a lot. These corners are chipped to hell."

Chase makes a living as a carpenter for his dad's company. He's picky when it comes to furniture. It's borderline obnoxious, actually.

"Screw you," Eric says. "Not all of us come from money or get paid what we're worth. I work hard for the shitty things I have, thank you very much."

Chase holds up his hands. "No judgment. Just stating the obvious. I can refurbish everything if you want me to."

"And how much is that gonna cost me?"

He laughs and leans forward. "I'll make you a deal, I'll fix the coffee table for free in exchange for a new side piece. I'll choose a girl from your contacts list, and you introduce me to her at your next party."

"There's no shortage of females in your phone. Call up one of them."

"I want someone new. Don't get it twisted, though. She's gotta be single and platonic where you're concerned. I'm not looking to turn our bromance into an eskimo brothers thing. You've got plenty of female friends. I don't." He turns to look at me. "Other than you, of course."

"Nice save," I tease.

He gently bumps his shoulder into mine and refocuses his attention on Eric. "Start scrolling."

"If I introduce you to a homegirl, you keep it one hundred with her. Make it abundantly clear what you're looking for. I don't need any extra drama between friends. And no going back on your word if she's not into you, either. You get one shot, and one shot only."

"Duly noted."

Eric blows out an exasperated breath and raises his hips to retrieve his phone from his back pocket. He swipes the screen and sifts through his contacts, showing Chase profile photos of the girls for feedback.

"Next," Chase dismisses.

"What about her?"

"Pass."

Eric's list of female contacts is endless. I knew it was extensive, but this is absurd. My grip on the ice pack tightens infinitesimally. Thinking about him with other girls brings out my jealous streak. I don't want him to suspect anything, so I play it cool and keep my emotions bottled.

"Whoa, hold up. Who's she?"

Eric looks at the screen. "Mia Foster."

"She's cute."

Before I can squash Chase's intrigue, Eric beats me to the punch. "She's a no-go, dude. She only lives here for the summer."

"Even better."

"Absolutely not," I interject. "She isn't just Eric's friend, she's mine. Besides, she doesn't do casual hookups. Pick someone else."

It's nothing against Chase, but I don't want him using Mia. She's got enough problems to deal with back home. This is the one time during the year she can let loose. She doesn't need boy problems spoiling her fun.

"Cockblockers," Chase mutters.

The slideshow continues. Somewhere in the middle, my arm begs for a break. I get up and walk over to the kitchen and drain the loose water from the bottom of the Ziploc bag. I open the freezer up and fill it with more ice, then rewrap it in a hand towel and return to my spot on the coffee table just in time for them to finish up their stupid little wager.

Chase's phone buzzes. He glances down to read the text.

"Uh...change of plans, guys. Gotta bounce."

I turn my head. "Are you serious? You're ditching us?"

"Afraid so."

He stands and finishes his beer. This has to be a booty call. He wouldn't be in such a hurry for any other reason. I'm surprised, but I can't say I'm disappointed. Ultimately, this works out in my favor. Eric and I need to have a conversation and figure out how to resolve our issues without Chase lurking around.

"Thanks for saving my ass tonight," Eric tells him.

"Sure thing. I'll text you tomorrow," Chase replies, setting the empty bottle on the kitchen counter. "Raven, always a pleasure."

"See ya later. Thanks again for all your help," I respond.

"Anytime."

As soon as the door closes, Eric's sharp blue eyes find mine. Uncertainty and silence fill the empty space between us. It's sobering. All it does is remind me how fractured we really are. I'm emotionally exhausted, and we haven't even cracked the surface of our issues yet.

With all the extra time I've had to think over the last few days, I've realized something important. No matter how much Eric thinks he's ready for a relationship, he's not. Pursuing me is one thing, committing to me is another. He wants sex and companionship without the burden of intimacy. That's a deal breaker. I'm not willing to compromise and beg for scraps. I meant it when I said I wanted a real, honest friendship over a phony relationship. His lack of effort and fleeting affection can go to someone else. As much as it kills me to imagine that possibility, the alternative is worse.

Question is, what comes next?

Before I can verbalize the thought, he rests his hand on my upper thigh, distracting me. A jolt of heat shoots up my leg and settles on my sweet spot. I blink, trying to concentrate on icing his wounds. His fingertips lightly dance over my skin, stirring a rush of excitement inside me. No other guy has ever made me feel this way. It's fantasy-shrouding insanity. If that's what's in store for me, sign me up for a straitjacket. As long as it's custom-made with Italian leather, I'm in.

My body is charged, humming with desire, acutely aware of everything that's happening. His fingers glide higher. Before I lose any and all common sense, I slap his hand away and deny him access.

"Ah! You're adding to my injuries."

"If you'd learn to keep your hands to yourself, you wouldn't have any injuries."

He grins proudly. "I did it all for you."

"I didn't ask you to."

His smile falters. He runs both hands through his hair, visibly aggravated. "I can't win with you, can I?"

I rest the ice pack on my lap and assess his wounds. The bleeding has stopped but the swelling looks the same. "I appreciate you sticking up for me—really, I do—but you shouldn't have hit him. That's taking it too far. I'm perfectly capable of defending myself. You don't need to jump in and manhandle the situation like Mike Tyson. What if the cops had shown up? What if Levi presses charges? Or worse yet, what if you'd ended up in the hospital? You could've been seriously hurt because of me."

"No, not because of you. Because of Levi and his big mouth. He was out of line, so I put him back in his place. End of story. I stand by my actions. The price I paid was worth it—all of it. Even losing him as a friend. I'm not saying it wasn't a reckless thing to do, but it sure as hell wasn't pointless."

"Eric, I don't want to be the reason why you get hurt or wind up in these scenarios. If I hadn't been there tonight, none of this would've happened. I should've followed my instincts and stayed home."

"None of this is your fault. Quit making it about you. He's the one who made the comment, and I'm the one who lost it and retaliated. Big deal. Shit happens. No use in blaming yourself or analyzing it to death. It'll drive you crazy until you deflect or self-destruct. Those are my traits. Capiche? Don't go stealing them. You're the dramatic one, I'm the impulsive one. That's how this works. It's way too late in the game for switching."

I suppress a smile and drop my gaze. I stare impassively at the ice pack in my lap. When I lift my head again, my expression is replaced with sympathy. "I'm sorry you lost a friend tonight."

His eyes soften. "It is what it is. It's not like I didn't see it coming."

Knowing that information doesn't make me feel any better. As much as I couldn't stand Levi, I didn't want Eric to lose another person in his life. He's already had enough people skip out on him. How does someone who's been through so much abandonment learn to trust? No wonder he's afraid of getting attached. And who can blame him? I may be willing to put myself out there, but it doesn't make it any less scary. That's what life's all about, though—taking chances and sharing your journey with people who enhance you. Forget about wanting someone to complete you. That's overrated. You need to be able to stand on your own as a strong individual. Someone should always add to who you are, not make you who you are.

Speaking of standing on your own....

"What did you mean earlier when you said you aren't sure what you're capable of giving me anymore?"

A few beats of silence pass. He leans forward and exhales a breath so heavy my hair sways. All signs are pointing to another major letdown. As if my heart could take another trampling.

Sayonara remission.

"You have no idea how much I want us to be together, but I can't give you what you want. That's already been proven. You need full disclosure about my past, and I'm not willing to give it. We each have certain expectations for what we want out of a relationship. Problem is they're not matching up. Thursday night was a wake-up call. I've never seen you get so angry to the point where we're not communicating. It made me realize I'm not willing to jeopardize the friendship again. If the stakes weren't so high, I would've had you a long time ago, so don't mistake anything I'm saying for regret. I wouldn't take back a single moment with us, even in hindsight. You're my girl. Always have been. Always will be. But please understand I can't afford to lose you."

It's taking every ounce of courage I have not to break down and cry. I feel like he just poured a bucket of acid over my heart and he's watching it slowly corrode away when he's the one who should be protecting it. In all our years of playing catch and release, he's never been the one to reject me. How did he survive this repeatedly? It feels like my entire world is collapsing. Deep down I know he's right, but it doesn't make this any less painful. "Are you breaking up with me?" I half joke. "'Cause it sure sounds like a breakup, and we're not even dating."

He grabs my chin and uses his thumb to caress the side of my cheek. I can't tell if the gesture makes everything hurt more, or less.

I'm just trying to get through this conversation in one piece. "I blame your age."

"Why?"

"Because if you weren't so young when I first met you, and you hadn't made yourself indispensable, this probably would have worked out."

*This probably would have worked out…*meaning it's never going to? I know the timing isn't right, but he's making it seem like we don't ever stand a chance. He's setting us up for failure before we even get out of the starting blocks.

Why did I have to fall for this emotionally unavailable guy? What does that say about me? I'm not attracted to Eric because he needs to be fixed, but I'd be lying if I said the bad boy persona wasn't thrilling. He's an all or nothing kinda guy, which is what attracted me to him in the first place—well, that and those clear sky eyes—but it's also why he won't commit to me. He can't give me his all.

"Why do we keep doing this to ourselves? You and me, we fit. We've been into each other for years, and we've been burying our feelings and coming up with excuse after excuse not to act on them. First it's my age, then it's poor timing, then it's casual flings, or fear of intimacy, fear of dependency, blah blah blah. It never ends. How long are we going to stay on the merry-go-round? Because it never seems to stop spinning and I'm not sure how much longer I can hold on." I catch my breath and finish off my final thought. "I don't understand why I'm not worth a fair shot."

His response nearly crushes me.

"Because I meant it when I said you weren't like any other girl."

Wow. What a way to throw that back in my face.

"You know we're not ready. You deserve more," he says, studying my reaction.

"You can't say for certain we wouldn't last."

"And you can't guarantee we will," he counters.

"I'll never be able to guarantee anything. Life doesn't work that way. But at least I'm willing to fight for the people who matter most to me. I'm scared too, you know, but I don't let my fear cripple me."

I don't know why I'm arguing the issue. He isn't saying anything untrue. The timing isn't right. Until he learns to open up, we're always going to be a recipe for disaster. But it feels so final, so permanent. He's taking the option away without my consent. All that does is make me want it more.

I have no idea how much times passes before he speaks again.

"It'll happen for us one day, Rave. I promise."

Part of me resents him for thinking he's the one who gets to call all the shots in this relationship. I'm not implying I should have all the control, but neither should he. He's delusional if he thinks I'm going to sit on the sidelines and wait while he partakes in all the action.

"What does this mean for us? And where do we go from here?"

He shrugs. "We do what we've always done."

"Pretend?"

"No," he frowns. "We be there for each other no matter what."

Or in other words, pretend. What a colossal waste of my time. I'm swearing off guys for the rest of eternity. If this is even a fraction of how it would feel to be in a real, no holds barred relationship, I have no desire to be in one. We've run around in circles, only to end up right back where we started. At this point I'd rather deny myself what I want outright. Anything to avoid hanging around in lovey-dovey limbo for one more second.

Abruptly, he stands and offers his hand.

"Come."

I look up at him, confused. "Where are we going?"

"For a swim."

I check the clock on his microwave. It's already past eleven.

"Now?"

He nods and sticks his hand farther out, prompting me.

"But I don't have a swimsuit."

"You don't need one."

"I am not skinny dipping with you."

He grins and lets his heated gaze appraise my body. "As fun as that would be, who said anything about skinny dipping?"

I glance down at the dress I'm wearing. "You want me to swim in this?"

He waggles his eyebrows suggestively.

"Cut that out. You don't get to be all flirty if you're not going to follow it up with something long-term. Stop sending mixed signals."

"Fair enough. Let's go."

I place my hand in his and let him lead me outside to the pool. The temperature's perfect for a midnight swim—comfortable, and not too humid. Crickets and katydids sound off in the night. A trail of glowing lights helps pave the way to the pool.

When we reach the chaise lounges, I remove my heels and jewelry, and claim a spot. Eric slips his tee over his head and tosses it onto the chair next to mine. He deftly unbuttons his jeans and slides them down his legs. I focus my attention on the water in front of me. It's calming. When I turn around to face him again, I try to ignore the fact that he's standing before me in a pair of navy boxer briefs. *So much for the calm factor.* He digs through his jean pockets and pulls out a Zippo and a joint.

My eyes widen. "Eric, what are you doing?"

"Relax. No one's out here."

"Where'd you get that?"

"I bummed one from Levi's party."

I'm not oblivious to the fact that he smokes occasionally, but he's never brought it around me. I honestly don't know how to feel about it. Half of me is curious to find out what all the hype is about, and the other half is filled with a nagging paranoia. He studies my reaction and slips the joint behind his ear, his lips curving into a sly grin.

"Sometimes I forget how innocent you are."

I look down and feel my cheeks heat. I hate being perceived as a goody-goody. I want to be fun and carefree, not uptight and self-righteous. There's got to be a happy medium, right? It's not like anyone's ever died from smoking pot. And I'm a firm believer in trying something at least once. As long as you're not hurting anybody, what's the big deal?

The sound of Eric's voice cuts through my dilemma. "If it makes you uncomfortable, I'll hold off until later."

I shake my head and flip my hair over my shoulder. "No, it's fine. Can I try?"

"If you want to."

He throws his jeans on the chaise lounge and beckons me over.

My legs move until I'm standing two feet in front of him. He retrieves the joint from behind his ear and rests it between his lips. He flicks the Zippo until a burning flame sparks to life and leans forward to light the tip. I glance around and quadruple-check to make sure no one's watching us. He takes a hefty drag, holds his breath for a few beats, and flips the cap shut. He turns to blow the smoke away from my face.

He passes me the joint. I examine it carefully. "How do I do this?"

"It's simple. Take a hit and hold it as long as you can."

Sounds simple enough.

I look into his eyes and slip the joint between my lips. Timidly, I inhale. A deep burn spreads through my chest. Feels like my lungs are incinerating. I hold it for all of two seconds before I'm coughing profusely.

He chuckles and snatches the joint from my fingers. "If you're coughing on your first time, you're doing it right."

I grip my chest. "How can anyone enjoy that?"

"You get used to it. Just wait until the effects set in."

My mouth tastes like moldy ass. I don't know which is worse, the taste or the smell. He takes a second hit and offers me another drag. I accept. Might as well reap the benefits and make it worth the experience.

I inhale and pass it off. "How much do I have to smoke in order to get high?"

"Since it's only your first time, a couple hits will be plenty."

"Thank God."

He laughs and finishes off the joint in a matter of minutes. I mosey over to the edge of the pool and dip my toes in the water, secretly thanking my lucky stars that I wore a red dress tonight instead of a white one.

"So I was thinking—"

My sentence is cut off when Eric barrels into me from behind and catapults us belly-first into the pool. Cool water revitalizes every inch of me, temporarily washing away all my troubles. I'm weightless and free. My dark hair billows around me and my dress clings like a second skin.

I break the surface and suck in a deep breath. Before I can rip Eric a new one, he submerges himself, grabs my legs, and yanks me back under. I try to fight him off but he spreads my thighs apart and pulls me toward him until they're wrapped around his torso. He plants his hands firmly on the small of my back and brings us both up for air.

"What did I say about the flirting? Do you not pay attention to anything I say to you anymore?"

"Not really," he responds.

I know it'll hurt so much more in the long run, but I can't make myself stop wanting this. I love our close proximity and the feel of his hands on me. I love the way he's looking at me—like he can't make himself stop, either. It's addictive and maddening.

He reaches up and uses the pad of his thumb to wipe away the mascara streaks under my eyes. I mentally chastise myself for not applying the waterproof kind.

"Have you decided what you're going to major in once college starts?"

I shake my head. "I want to pursue fashion, but it's not practical. I'm thinking business for starters, then design school. I'll need to know the business side of things anyway, so I may as well put myself through that. Once that's behind me, I can focus on what I really love."

"Just promise me you won't give up on your passion. I don't want society polluting your mind. You've wanted to design for so long."

"I won't. It's important to understand the ins and outs of starting my own line. I want to learn every aspect from top to bottom. Hopefully it'll pay off in the end."

"It will," he assures me. "You're one of the brightest people I know and you have an amazing eye for detail. No doubt you'll be successful in whatever you do."

A slow smile spreads across my face. "You're the best confidence booster, you know that?"

"Ditto," he says, then kisses me on the lips without warning.

My heart swells. I stop him. "No kissing allowed! Do I have to spell it out for you?"

He laughs. His hands squeeze me tighter, making me feel even more exceptional. On a crude note, I'm certain he can feel me nipping out.

Whatever, he loves it.

I can't pinpoint exactly when it happens, but somewhere along the way, time lapses. It feels like we have forever and a day to experience this moment. I lean forward and kiss him, despite all my reservations. This time it's gradual. We forget about everything and focus solely on getting lost in each other. Our tongues collide, sending shivers up my spine. His lips are slick and smooth, moving effortlessly with mine. My fingers tangle in his wet hair. He grips my backside and presses me closer. A low moan rips through my throat.

I know we're prolonging the inevitable, but for a brief moment I'm able to pretend like I'm not expecting anything more. I allow the illusion to manifest and carry me through. What if I never feel this way about anyone else? What if nobody understands me like him? I don't believe in soul mates, but I do know there's only one Eric.

Conflicted, I break the kiss and rest my forehead against his, listening to the sound of our ragged breaths.

"Now who's sending mixed signals?" he asks, humor gleaming in his eyes.

Instead of answering him, I fall back into a floating position with my legs still secured around his waist. I spread my arms out and stare up at the starry night sky.

I unhook my legs from his torso and crouch down to blow bubbles on the surface of the water. Reminds me of being a kid and blowing bubbles in my chocolate milk. Eric splashes me in the face, causing a serious case of the giggles.

I hold onto the edge of the pool and try to catch my breath. "I think I'm high."

Both his brows shoot up. "Ya think?"

"I feel weird."

"Good weird or bad weird?"

"Different weird."

"Excellent clarification."

"I know, right?"

We spend the next several hours swimming, philosophizing about nothing, gorging on peanut butter pancakes, watching hilarious YouTube videos, and listening to Alanis Morissette on repeat. Eric begged for a different band choice, but I vetoed his request. He wouldn't stop flirting. The score had to be settled somehow. Around 3:00 a.m. we crash on his couch. Walking all the way to his bedroom seemed like too much work. I've never slept so well.

/

All in all, it was a fantastic start to the summer. We made unforgettable memories and conquered milestones together. We kept our complicated situation under wraps, stealing forbidden kisses when no one was looking. We thrived on the secrecy at first, but the more we messed around, the harder it became to fool ourselves into thinking we could make it out unscathed.

Still, Eric wouldn't budge when it came to crossing that boundary, which I took to mean we were going ultra-slow. I thought if given enough time, he'd eventually commit. Imagine my surprise when he landed his first official girlfriend (not me) by the time autumn rolled around. Devastation doesn't even begin to cover how I felt.

Everything changed overnight. We went back to being just friends, but it was never the same. No matter how hard I tried to bury my feelings, they wouldn't completely go away. That's what scared me the most. I'd become so infatuated, so consumed by him, that I lost my sense of self. Never again. My only saving grace was college. I spent the majority of my first semester buried deep in design sketches and dull classes like Business Finance and Statistics. Pouring all my heartache into my dream was the only way I could repair the damage. After all, this was my fault. Can't say Eric didn't warn me. Plus, I'm the one who insisted I'd rather see him give his fleeting affection to someone else over me. If I couldn't have it all, I didn't want anything.

Word of advice: when someone tells you to be careful what you wish for, take that one to heart.

ELEVEN

r a v e n

Three Years Later....

I glance down and check the time on my phone while my date, Devin, continues to spew politics, repeatedly shoving his viewpoints straight down my throat. Everything from immigration to our economy is up for debate. Since when are these appropriate conversation starters for a first date? I've taken enough business classes to know exactly what's going on with our economy. I don't need the hour-long recap. Unfortunately for me, no matter how bored I appear to be, this guy isn't getting the memo.

Just as I'm debating a clean exit, Devin reaches across the table and steals my untouched glass of pinot noir. He gulps it down without a second thought, leaving me momentarily dazed by his odd behavior.

By all means, help yourself.

He pops a couple buttons on his shirt and uses the fabric to fan himself. "Is it hot in here, or is it just me?"

"Uh, I'm going to go out on a limb and say it's the entire bottle of wine you drained."

"We split it."

"I had one glass, and you just inhaled my second one."

"I thought you were finished...?"

Another blind date gone awry. I'm going to kill Tori for setting me up with this one. The only reason I agreed to go out with this guy in the first place is because I wanted to put her concerns to rest. Ever since she moved out and ditched me for San Marcos last year, she's been keeping close tabs on my love life. She doesn't want my vagina to dry up. Her words, not mine. She says it's already accumulated dust, and the next stage is some kind of petrification. Truth is my heart's not in the dating game. I'm far too busy with school, work, and my internship.

Out of the corner of my eye, I catch the server walking by. I hold a finger up to silence Devin and flag him like my life depends on it. "Excuse me, can we get the check, please?"

"Certainly. Will this all be on one ticket?"

Devin looks at me quizzically.

Oh, *now* he wants to be progressive?

Our server glances back and forth between the two of us. The air thickens with awkward tension. We obviously didn't discuss who gets to pay beforehand. I believe the person who asked for the date should pay. Problem is we were both set up by Tori, so technically no one asked.

"Let's put it all on mine," Devin reluctantly says.

I nod my approval. Our server removes our plates and disappears.

Devin leans forward. "This was a total bust, wasn't it?"

I shrug and rotate the stem of my empty wine glass between my fingers. Guess he was picking up on the signs all along.

"The food was good." I wince as soon as the words leave my mouth. I finish off the last of my water, hoping to wash down the guilt, and place my linen on the table. "Do you need a ride home?"

He slumps back against his chair and rubs his hands up and down his face. "Man, I should've known a girl like you couldn't hold an intellectual conversation."

Not exactly the answer I was looking for. Color me offended. Note to self: next time just seek out someone for casual sex. No need to go through all of this. If I were a more spiteful person, I'd make Devin drive himself home. But I can't do that in good conscience.

The server drops off the check, which saves me from having to sit through any more of this shitshow. I whip two fives out of my purse and slap them down on the table.

Devin looks up and frowns.

"For the tip," I clarify. "Let's go. I'm driving you home. And once you make it inside your apartment, you're going to do us both a favor and lose my number."

He tries to protest but refrains when he sees the irritated expression on my face. He opens the booklet and slides a fifty inside, plus my two fives. We stand up and gather our things, then he follows me out to my car.

/

"He did what?!"

"You heard me. The bastard blew chunks all over my upholstery. Only thing worse would've been if it had landed on my shoes. No more blind dates, Tori. I mean it. You've been demoted back to my BFF only."

"Hey, don't blame me. I'm an excellent matchmaker. It's not my fault your walls are impossible to breach."

I don't miss the double meaning in her words.

"This has nothing to do with my vagina and everything to do with his mouth. Specifically, all the crap that was spewing out of it—before *and* during the barf fest."

"You're being dramatic."

"There was red wine. How am I supposed to get that stain out?"

"Oh, my God," she starts laughing hysterically.

"It's not funny. It's disgusting. The passenger floor reeks of garlic and salmon."

That one makes her laugh even harder. "Stop it. Can't...breathe," she gasps.

I pinch the bridge of my nose, fighting to hold back my own laughter. "It was so bad. He was boring me to death with political viewpoints before we even got our salads."

"You know it's bad when his upchuck reflexes are the highlight of the whole evening."

"Tell me about it. First dates should be light and fun. Feeling each other out and whatnot. I was there to have a good time, not sit through Macroeconomics."

"You should've pulled out a pen and paper and started taking notes."

I laugh and walk up the steps to my apartment. When I reach the door, I cradle the phone against my cheek and fiddle with my keys. "Hey, I'm home and want to change. Can I call you back in a bit?"

"Sure thing."

"Sweet. Talk to you later."

"Okay. Bye."

I end the call and unlock my door. Leftover chocolate zucchini bread caresses my senses. The urge to throw on an apron and bake everything in my kitchen hit me out of nowhere this morning. A common side effect of that Bellotti-bred blood.

I slip out of my heels and toss my purse and keys on the counter. Sauntering into the kitchen, I break off a chunk of zucchini bread and close my eyes, savoring the taste. Details from tonight's poor excuse for a date start replaying through my mind, effectively killing my appetite.

Seriously, what was Tori thinking?

Before I have a chance to get all fired up again, my phone vibrates in my purse.

"Hello?"

Sniffling sounds register.

"Mia? What's wrong?"

I hear a muffled sob, followed by, "It's my mom. I don't think I can do this anymore, Rave."

I figured this would happen sooner or later. Nancy's alcoholism has been an ongoing theme for years. It was only a matter of time before she broke Mia down completely. When Mia's dad died a couple years ago, everything imploded.

"What happened?"

"We got into a huge fight and she kicked me out of the house again."

"Are you staying at Hadley's?"

"Yeah, but she leaves tomorrow morning for a family vacation. I'm screwed."

"No, you're not. Pack your bags and drive down here."

Mia goes silent on the other end, then exhales harshly. "You know I can't come down and visit. There's no way I'll get the time off work."

"I'm not talking about coming to visit. I'm talking about moving down here."

Another round of silence.

"You can't be serious."

"Why not? It's the perfect solution. I have an empty bedroom waiting to be filled, and you need a place to stay. You already know the area. Plus, you've got Eric and me to lean on. I know it's not the same as having your dad here, but it's something."

"It's more than something," she acknowledges, "but it's crazy. I can't drop everything and leave. Besides, I don't want to burden you with all my shit."

"Mia, I hate to break it to you, but things aren't going to get better. No one should have to sacrifice this much at twenty-two. It's ridiculous. And no self-respecting parent would ever do that to her own child. You need your freedom, and I need more Mia in my life. Make that happen. What do you have to lose?"

She's considering my proposal; I can feel it.

"If I do this, I won't be able to pay you rent right away. My savings is almost drained from all the bills my mom owes."

"That's fine. Just get down here. Once you get situated, we'll find you a job and go from there."

I can sense the immediate relief on the other end of the line. It's so monumental, it hits me all the way down here in Texas.

"There's chocolate zucchini bread," I bribe.

She exhales. "Screw it. Let's do this. Can I move in next weekend? I need to finish out the remainder of my shifts at the diner and the café. I don't want to screw anyone over. They've all been so good to me."

"I have to work Saturday and Sunday, but I'll see if I can swap a shift with Emilio on one of those days so I can be here to help move you in."

"Do you work Friday?"

"No, but I have class until 1:15."

"I'll have to drive all day anyway, so let's shoot for Friday night if you're free."

"Works for me."

"Oh, my God. Thank you so much, Rave. Seriously, you have no idea what you've just done for me."

A wide grin sweeps across my face. "I'm getting just as much out of this arrangement as you are. Two single chicks on the loose? Uh...yes, pretty mama."

She laughs and I can't help but wonder how long it's been since she's had something to laugh about.

"Maybe you can house sit for Hadley's fam? That way you have a place to stay until you come down here," I suggest.

"No way. I'm not asking them for help. It's not their responsibility to take care of me. I'll figure something out. Knowing there's light at the end of the tunnel makes everything worth it."

I exit the kitchen and stride into Mia's soon-to-be bedroom. I flip on the light and inspect the carpet to see if it needs vacuuming. I've only set foot in here once since Tori left, and that was to check and make sure she didn't leave anything behind.

"If you get in a bind and need to come down sooner, text me. The spare room is yours for as long as you need it."

"I don't even know if this is gonna work."

"Us living together?"

"No. Me starting over."

"Start by packing one box at a time. If it's not what you imagined once you get here, you can always go back. It's not a permanent decision unless you want it to be. Remember that later when you're torturing yourself with doubt."

She exhales. "You're right. I got this. I don't know why I'm so scared to pull the plug. It's not like anyone's taking care of me financially. I've proven I can make it on my own. Everything else pales in comparison."

"Exactly. Now hurry up and get down here."

Mia moved in the following Friday. To celebrate, we shimmied our way through one of Eric's ritualistic, lowbrow house parties and consumed more grilled hot dogs and beer than I'd care to admit to. Eric was stoked to see Mia, as always, but much to our amusement, she was busy flirting with someone else throughout the night— Chase.

Go figure.

I didn't even see the point in trying to prevent it. She can handle herself. Plus, Chase has eased his manwhore streak. Underneath that once shallow exterior resides a newly reformed human being. I'm trusting him not to screw my best friend over.

That same best friend is currently chilling out on my couch, scrolling through her phone, anxiously waiting for dinner. I stir the pasta and sample the sauce to see if it needs any more seasoning.

Glad I did that. I chop up some more basil and toss it into the pot to simmer. I switch on the light to the oven and bend down to check the status of the garlic bread.

"Do you think it's true that men think about sex every seven seconds?"

I straighten my spine and turn to look at Mia. "You're so random, you know that?"

"For real, though. Let that sink in. That's an obscene amount. There's no way they'd ever be able to get anything done during the day. Let's give them a little more credit."

"That sounds like an exaggeration," I agree.

"I'm going to get to the bottom of this."

She sits up on the couch and types furiously on her phone, hunting down answers.

"So, apparently there was a recent study conducted at Ohio State University where they had both men and women use clickers to record how often they each thought about sex, food, and sleep throughout the day."

"And?"

"According to this article, they found that the average man thought about sex 19 times a day, and the average woman thought about it 10 times a day. Men also thought about food and sleep more."

"Sounds legit."

"Yeah, but it begs the question: Were the participants holding back? I mean, if you were asked to be honest about every sexual thought you had, would you cop to it in a study?"

"Where is all this coming from?" I ask, amused.

"When Chase and I were on our date the other night, I swear he thought about stripping me naked the whole time. And that's not me being conceited. I could see it in his eyes."

"What about you?"

"Oh, I was definitely entertaining the possibility. No question."

"Okay. So?"

"So it got me thinking. Was his reaction due to the fact that I was sitting right there for visual stimulation? Or are these images constantly playing through his mind?"

"It's because a hot girl was sitting directly across from him," Eric announces, kicking the front door shut behind him.

Mia looks up at him in disbelief. "The hell? You could hear us talking from the other side of the door?"

"Uh, yeah," he says like it's a no-brainer. "Y'all are loud. As soon as I heard the word sex, I stopped everything to eavesdrop."

Mia looks over at me, mouth all agape. I shrug and concentrate on stirring the sauce.

Eric leans down to drop a kiss on Mia's head, then strides over to do the same with me.

"Smells delicious," he praises. "Is there enough for me?"

"I wasn't put on this planet to cater to your every dire need, Eric."

He takes a considerable step back. "Well, excuse me, Gloria Steinem. Are you planning on serving me some food with that sass? Or do I have to fork over both balls in order to get a plate?"

"Don't start," I warn.

I have zero patience for his hate-flirting these days.

"You started it the moment I walked through the door. I've done nothing to you. Pause and reset, or I'm leaving."

"You two act like a married couple sometimes, I swear."

I stiffen.

Eric spins around. "Interesting observation, Mia. Let's review the facts, shall we? I never seem to do anything right, I'm constantly getting bitched at, we aren't having sex, and she finds me childish and incorrigible. Sounds about right. But at least with marriage you get the tax breaks," he sneers.

Irritated doesn't even begin to describe what I'm feeling. My face is as red as the spaghetti sauce. If looks could kill, he'd be dead right now.

Eric eases up, noticing my hostility. I inhale a deep breath. I've been so focused on not letting my true feelings slip that I've gone too far in the opposite direction. Now I'm snapping at him for no reason. It's always been a struggle to keep my emotions in check when he's around. You'd think I'd be a pro with all the practice I've had, but it's only gotten progressively worse. The more time passes, the more I find myself coming undone. Like someone gradually tugging on the loose thread of a sweater until it completely unravels.

"Are you coming to ACL with us this weekend, Strawberry?"

Mia glances back and forth between Eric and me, then nods.

"Yeah. Raven pitched the idea to me a couple days ago."

"Want to ride along with me? I'm heading down there for the morning shows and making it an all-day drinking and jamming extravaganza. Be my guiding light. Save me from the pathetic, miserable existence that is my life. Well, save me from existing alone in it, the *patheticness* of it all."

I roll my eyes.

"Jesus. Next time warn me before you go dark," Mia tells him.

"Is that a no?"

"No, I'll go with you. Chase offered to give me a ride, but I'll just text him and tell him I'm riding with you instead. Besides, he and Raven won't be able to make it until the evening."

"Solid. Everybody wins."

Beep! Saved by the timer. I strain the spaghetti and slip on some oven mitts to retrieve the garlic bread. Mia hops up and waltzes into the kitchen, grabbing us plates and silverware.

"And that's my cue to leave," Eric declares, twirling his keys around his index finger.

I glance over at him. "You're not staying?"

"Not unless you remove that Texas-sized chip on your shoulder."

"Rich coming from you."

"That's what I thought," he says, drifting toward the door. And he's gone.

A wave of disappointment washes over me. I'd be lying if I said I didn't want him to stay, but begging is for amateurs. Why can't he just step up and fight for me? Whatever. It's probably for the best. Wouldn't want to break the torturous cycle we have going and actually come to a resolution. What would be the fun in that?

TWELVE

r a v e n

I've never been one for large crowds. Too much chaos and claustrophobia. Having said that, if you're willing to surrender yourself to a predominantly hipster population with questionable fashion judgment, Austin City Limits Music Festival is the way to do it. Everything's spacious, outdoors, and low-key. Perfect combination for all day drinking and lounging with friends. You can listen to all the hottest bands and still manage to hold a semi-coherent conversation, depending on how hammered you are.

Too bad I'm the DD tonight.

When you're the most responsible one of the group, everyone looks to you for money, rides, guidance, support, and logical decision-making. Then, when they all sober up, they berate you for "mommying" them. Need someone to hold your hair while you puke your guts out? I'm your girl. Need to be bailed out of jail? Dial my number. Yup, that's me. Loyal and reliable to a fault. You make the mess; I'll clean it up.

Don't ask me how I'm always the one drafted for this position. It's a mystery. As if I'm incapable of having any fun myself.

I brush off my stormy mood and focus on finding my friends in a crowd of thousands. The heat is positively blistering. A cold anything sounds pretty good right about now. I finally come face to face with Mia and confess, "I need a drink."

"Rough night at the restaurant?"

"Very."

"Should we make it a double?"

"No. I'm driving tonight," I remind her.

"Oh, right. Good call."

We head toward one of the beer tents.

"Let's stop at the bathrooms on the way," she says.

"Broke the seal, did you?"

She nods gravely, causing me to laugh.

Mood improved.

After we purchase our beers, we weave through the masses, searching for Chase and Eric. We reach the stage where Foster the People is currently belting out "Are You What You Want To Be?" We stop to mingle and watch from a distance, taking it all in. I sip on my beer and barely avoid colliding with the person next to me. Once the song's over, we move on to a less crowded area and scan.

"I don't see them anywhere!" Mia yells in my ear.

"Me neither!"

Off to the side, I finally spot Eric and Chase enjoying the AWOLNATION show. My smile falters when I notice two attractive girls hanging around them. *Ugh.* Why am I not surprised? Is it impossible to leave these guys alone for five freaking seconds? I tug on Mia's arm and nod in their direction. She follows my line of vision.

The blonde hanging off Eric proceeds to wrap her arms around his neck and leans into his chest. She rises up on her tiptoes to say something in his ear. My jealousy flares.

"What the fuck is she doing?"

Mia spins around and shoots me a confused look.

"Seriously, why is he even entertaining the thought of her? He's supposed to be with me. Clueless idiot!" I shout.

Mia glances back and forth between Eric and me, clearly not picking up on the vibe. Suddenly, the entire picture falls into focus, creating a clear-cut image. No use in hiding it anymore. She's privy to what everyone else has known all along. I can tell she's hurt by the newfound knowledge.

She crosses her arms over her chest. "Rave, tell me what's going on. Now."

"Later," I mouth, my eyes pleading.

She drops her arms and shakes her head. I don't blame her for being upset. I should've told her a long time ago, but I didn't want her to feel torn between Eric and me. We're all she has down here.

I step forward and adjust both our outfits, so the boys have something to drool over. When I'm pleased, I grab her hand and power through the crowd.

"Come on. Whatever you do, don't let them see you sweat. That's giving them a satisfaction they don't deserve."

The guys sense our presence the moment we approach and spin around to face us. My guarded eyes find Eric's. I study his expression for any trace of guilt or longing and come up short on both counts. His hand slips around the blonde's waist possessively. He's testing me, itching to get under my skin. I smile sweetly, refusing to let him have it. If this is the way he wants to play it, I'll beat him at his own game.

"Are y'all going to introduce us to your friends, or are we just supposed to pull their names out of thin air?" I ask.

Chase and Eric glance at each other. Mia uses the opportunity to stare at me like I'm crazy. I shrug and give away nothing more.

"Mia, Raven, this is Tamika. Tamika works with me at Surge. This is her friend, Sasha," Chase motions to the girl around Eric's arm. "I was just telling her how surprised I was to see her here. I figured she was working the bar tonight, but she got the night off."

Mia and I step forward to shake both of the girls' hands.

I turn to focus my attention on Sasha.

"So, how do you know Eric?"

"I met him at Chase's place, actually. Tamika invited me over one night and we all hung out."

Mia stiffens when she hears that interesting tidbit. She's been on a date with Chase, just last week.

"Is that so?" I ask coyly. "Well, Mia and I were thinking about doing some bar hopping tonight to pick up some guys. Y'all should join. It'll be more fun as a group. What do you say, ladies?"

Tamika hesitates, her eyes darting back and forth between Chase and Eric. "Um, sure. Sounds like fun, I guess."

"Excellent!"

I can feel Eric's angry gaze burning a hole through the side of my head. I don't feel the least bit guilty. He'll get over it. Lord knows he's put me through similar situations.

For our last club of the night, we settle on Surge. It's packed wall-to-wall with tons of gorgeous guys, mood-setting lights, pulsating beats. We waste no time hitting the dance floor.

My prude complex shatters to a zillion pieces as I grind my hips provocatively into the guy who asked me to dance—the guy I've never seen before in my life. My mind screams not be *this* girl, but I ignore it. I'm sick of being good all the time. I want to let loose and have fun like everybody else.

When I catch Eric staring, I ramp it up. I want to gut him, make him suffer as much as he's made me suffer. Based on the look in his eyes, it's working. He retaliates by fisting the back of Sasha's hair and crushing his lips to hers.

Suddenly, I don't feel like dancing anymore.

I back up, stunned. Bastard is ballsier than I gave him credit for. I keep my eyes zeroed in on their lips, watching the man I love more than anything passionately kiss another woman. A sharp pang hits my chest. I force myself to stay put and absorb it. Remember it. I need this. Without it, I'll slip back into old patterns and forget all the reasons why I should stay away from him.

When I've had my fill, I wander off the dance floor and seek refuge in the girls' bathroom to purge my trapped tears. The chick in the stall next to me is puking. Every time I sniffle, she hurls. Quite melodic. What really sucks is I can't even get drunk to numb the pain. Can't a girl catch a break?

Why do I always let Eric get the best of me? And why can't I get him out of my head? Short of cutting him out of my life, I've tried everything. Nothing helps. Every guy who waltzes in and challenges that is nothing more than a temporary replacement. Terrible, but true.

Drunk Girl flushes the toilet, the stall door swings open, and she stumbles into the sink. This saves me from my own pity party; I should check to see if she's okay. Just as I decide to unlock my door, I hear, "Rave?"

I place my hands on either side of the stall and tilt my head back to stare at the ceiling, mentally cursing the sound of Mia's voice. I hate it when people see me crying like a hot mess. So not cute.

"I know it's you in there. I'd recognize those Brian Atwood knockoffs anywhere. Open up," she demands.

Time to woman up. "These are *not* knockoffs."

"Like I'd know. Got ya out here," she smiles.

Damn, I love her.

Drunk Girl slinks past Mia and exits the bathroom, leaving us alone to talk.

"What happened between you and Eric?"

"Which time?"

"Any time."

I sigh and glance at my haggard reflection in the mirror, barely recognizing the girl staring back. Since when is vengeance in my repertoire? I've always considered myself a lover, not a fighter. Maybe I'm not as wholesome as I thought.

"We don't have to talk about it if you don't want to," she reassures. "I just want to make sure you're okay."

"I'm working on it."

"Have you guys hooked up?"

My eyes find hers. I swallow and nod.

"Why didn't you tell me?"

"Long story. I swear I'll tell you everything tomorrow, but I can't tonight. I'm drained."

Without saying another word, she walks over and pulls me into a tight hug. I close my eyes to keep from crying all over again and squeeze her back.

"You know I'm here for you. You can talk to me about anything. Even Eric."

My body relaxes.

"I know. And I love you for it, baby girl."

She releases me and turns to grab the handle on the door. "Come on. Let's get out of here and go home. I'll ride with you."

"Did you and Chase work everything out?"

She bites her lip suggestively. "Maybe. You cool if he comes back to our place tonight, or do you need some space?"

"Depends. Is it going to be a chill session, or a Do Not Disturb session?"

She shrugs. "Haven't decided yet. Probably both."

I laugh and follow her out, feeling eternally grateful that friends like her exist in my life.

After a twenty-minute car ride filled with 19.5 minutes of boy bashing and thirty seconds of self-reflection, I've decided not to go down without a fight. Eric doesn't get to have the final word, or in this case, the last kiss (with some random blonde bombshell). I'm determined to settle the score by racing over to his apartment, breaking down his door, and beating the living shit out of him.

The moment I hear Mia hop in the shower, I grab my keys off the kitchen counter and beeline toward the front door to avoid an inquisition. If she knew what I was up to, she'd stop me. Especially after the way Eric treated me tonight. All the more reason to keep it moving.

Just before I reach the doorknob, three loud knocks resonate, scaring the crap out of me. I fling it open and come face to face with Chase.

"Mia's in the shower. She'll be out shortly. You can either hang out here or head into her room and wait. Either way, don't be a pervert about it."

I slip past him without waiting for a response.

On the way over to Eric's apartment, I rehearse all possible conversation starters—assuming he's home. Going in blind is risky business. I haven't even thought about how I'm going to react if Sasha's there. If I know him like I think I do, he'll already have her stripped naked and spread-eagled. Marvelous. Cockblocking is worth extra points.

I park the car and jump out. My heart is racing. I tell myself it's adrenaline leftover from my rage. It definitely has nothing to do with nerves or anticipation.

I bang on the door like a cop searching for a criminal. I hear shuffling sounds, followed by the deadbolt unlocking.

Eric opens the door and glares. "What do you want, Raven?"

He's fully clothed. There's no sign of Sasha, or any other girl for that matter.

Thank God.

I shove my hands against his chest.

He stumbles back a couple paces, then looks me up and down, angry and confused.

"What the hell is your problem?"

"You," I hiss, slamming the door shut behind me.

Before he can react, I push him up against the wall and seal my mouth over his.

There. That'll show him.

He secures my face between his hands and kisses me back, no holds barred. This kiss is ten times more potent than the one I watched earlier—one part hate, two parts love. And it's the best kiss I've ever had.

We stagger toward the bedroom but don't make it out of the living room. Best decision ever. His bedroom is a whole 'nother twelve steps away. May as well be twelve miles.

He breaks the kiss to ditch his shirt. He bunches it up in his hands and throws it at me. "You're such a fucking pain in my ass."

I resist the urge to slap him and drag his face back down to my lips. "And you're completely hopeless," I tell him.

He boosts me up. My legs reflexively wrap around his waist. We fall backwards into the couch, his weight nearly crushing me. He kisses me ardently and reaches down to massage me between my legs at the exact same moment his tongue plunges into my mouth. I moan appreciatively and grind against the pressure.

"Jesus Christ you're wet."

"Years of foreplay," I say breathlessly.

"I'll say."

Itching fingers slip into the waistband of my jeans and tug. "Take these off."

I offer my hips to him as an invitation. "You do it."

He runs a finger straight down the seam, making me squirm. "Gladly."

My shoes slip off. The jeans are next to go. He hovers over me and fists the hem of my cami in his hands, dragging it over my head.

I've never felt so desirable. Leave it to Eric to make me feel two polar extremes in one night.

He grabs my hips and brings me up so I'm straddling him. I brace myself against his chest to keep from falling over.

"Sit on my face and ride it," he commands.

My breath catches.

"Shouldn't we establish some boundaries first?"

"What have I told you about boundaries?" he growls.

Without giving me a chance to think, he slides my panties down just enough to expose me. The sultry, primal look on his face causes my sex to clench. I lift my hips and allow my eyes to close while he continues to push the delicate fabric down my thighs. Once it's out of his reach, I stand and shimmy the rest of the way.

He groans and slaps his forehead. "You're going to give me a fucking heart attack, woman."

I smile wickedly and climb back on top of him. I use my knees to inch forward and align the most intimate part of myself with his mouth. His hands grip the backs of my thighs. Slowly, deliberately, he eases me down onto his face. The moment his lips touch mine, I gasp.

He moans deeply and I feel it travel all the way up my spine. Sensory overload. The more he devours me, the faster my head spins.

My hips begin to move, desperately seeking that release. He slows his pace, keeping me on the brink. I reach for my clit but he blocks my advance and lifts me off his mouth. Before I can process what's happening, I'm on my back.

He stares down at me earnestly. "When you come, you're coming with me."

His body abandons mine and I make a frustrated noise. A chuckle escapes him as he deftly unfastens his jeans, then pushes them down and kicks them to the floor. He repeats the process with his boxers.

I swallow thickly. Even though we've done this before, it feels like the first time all over again. He hovers over me and presses the tip against my entrance. His eyes shift to mine, his face becoming serious.

"I'm clean, I swear. Haven't had sex in six months."

"*Six months?*"

He nods. "Been too busy pining for a girl who's had me from the very beginning."

"Really? Tell me about her."

He gradually starts to sink into me. "She's smart, beautiful, and annoying as hell."

"Keep talking like that and I won't let you put it in," I threaten.

He grins and pushes himself to the hilt. My back arches in response. Vivid memories come rushing back. I'd forgotten how amazing Eric feels inside me.

"Are you on the pill? Or do I have to pull out?"

"I'm on the pill."

He visibly relaxes.

"Best news I've heard in six months."

His torso begins to move fluidly, expertly. I succumb to the pleasure and ignore the small voice in the back of my head warning me this will never last. I'm not expecting anything beyond casual sex. I've learned my lesson. Eric may be the person I trust most with my body, but he's the person I trust least with my heart.

"Your head off somewhere else?"

Our gazes collide.

"Not at all."

"Better not be. I was prepared to kick this up a notch."

"Well, in that case…" I wrap my arms around his neck and pretend to drift off again.

"That's it. You asked for it."

He abruptly pulls out and flips me onto my stomach, then yanks my hips up and swiftly buries himself inside me again.

"Oh, God."

One of his hands grips my hip while the other one fists the back of my hair, keeping me right where he wants me. "You have a phenomenal ass. One day, I'm going to take that virginity too."

He eases back and pushes inside again, making me groan. I meet him thrust for thrust, establishing a rhythm.

"Are you close, baby?"

"Almost," I respond.

He increases the pace, causing my entire body to erupt in chills. We're determined to cross the finish line together. And when that glorious moment finally arrives, we fall apart in one piece, just like he promised.

THIRTEEN

eric

We're curled up on the couch watching *American Beauty* on Netflix. Her head is resting in my lap. My fingers are idly stroking her hair. Solid recipe for romance, right? Think again. Miss I-Have-A-Ball-Busting-Opinion-Every-Two-Seconds has been uncharacteristically quiet. We should've completed round two by now, but something's up. And I don't want to fuck this up again. Instead of spending another thirty minutes decoding the warped female psyche and coming up with my own assumptions, I go direct.

"What's on your mind?"

Easy question guaranteed to warrant a simple response.

"Life."

Or not.

"That's broad. Care to clarify?"

She shakes her head and keeps her attention fixated on the screen. This blasé attitude is getting on my nerves. Did I miss something? Just once I'd like to have sex when it's not precipitated or followed by an argument. Or in this case, both.

I reach for the Xbox controller and pause the movie.

"Are you having regrets about what just happened between us?"

"Not at all," she insists.

My fingers stop stroking her hair. Before I can call bullshit, her attention drifts to the wall where my mom's portrait is hanging. I study her reaction closely, searching for any sign that will clue me in to what she's thinking. She opens her mouth to say something, but ultimately decides against it.

"I don't have many photographs of her, so I drew one," I offer up.

"Why don't you have many photographs?"

"It's hard to capture meaningful moments when there weren't many to document in the first place."

She glances up at me. "Do you miss her?"

"Sometimes."

"Are you angry?"

I mull that one over.

"Not as much as I used to be. I've come to accept that she's the best version of herself she can possibly be."

She's quiet for a moment.

"How often do you see each other?"

"Not as often as we should," I admit.

"What about your dad?"

"What about him?" I say, brushing a stray hair away from her forehead. She closes her eyes, relishing the contact. When they reopen, there's a depth of yearning, a hunger for more information.

"Why isn't there any trace of him in your life?"

"Well, for starters, I've never met my biological father. The only semblance of a father I've ever known was my mom's boyfriend who helped 'raise' me. He ended up skipping out when things got rough."

"Do you know anything about your real dad?"

"Other than him raping my mom and leaving her pregnant with me at sixteen, not a thing."

"Jesus," she gasps, horrified.

"Yep. Now imagine being raised by a woman who never wanted you in the first place, who had absolutely no choice in the matter, and who had to constantly be reminded of that reality every time she looked at me—at you. One of the most traumatic experiences a person could ever survive resulted in my conception. In a weird way, I'm responsible for ruining her life. Combine that with a pseudo dad who had no legal or genetic claim to me, and a bunch of other dysfunctional shit, and you'll wind up with one really confused kid and two equally resentful parents."

She's silent for a few beats. I get it. I mean, what do you say to something like that, anyway?

"Eric, what happened to your mom was horrible, but if she truly didn't want you, she had alternatives. You have to believe you were wanted. All parents love their children. Some just have better ways of expressing it than others."

I laugh sardonically. "She tried to have me aborted, Rave. My grandparents wouldn't allow it. She was underage, and she needed parental consent. They refused to give it. Lucky for me, right?"

"Hey, stop it. None of this is your fault. You didn't ask for any of this to happen to you."

"Neither did my mom. She was a kid too. One with a bright future ahead of her until some asshole came along and raped her at a party."

This is such a bizarre situation to be stuck in. I can't be grateful for my own existence and still sympathize with my mom. Doesn't work that way. Being happy I'm here makes it seem like I'm condoning what happened to her. Then I feel guilty and worthless all over again. Such a mindfuck.

Raven sits up and swings a leg over to straddle me. She cups my face between her hands and forces me to meet her gaze. The level of intimacy being shared between us is uncomfortable. I don't bother to say anything, though. It's a better alternative to the blatant indifference she was giving me before.

"Listen, you may think you are the worst thing to happen to her, but you are without a doubt one of the best things to happen to me. And Chase. And Mia. Just because your parents failed to recognize how amazing you are doesn't mean no one else sees it, 'cause we all do. Having you in my life has made me a better person. Albeit, a crazier person, but a better one."

"Did you just crack a joke during a serious conversation?" I reach up and feel her forehead. The woman must be sick if she's using my favorite defense mechanism to lighten the mood.

She slaps my hand away and wraps her arms around my neck. "I took a chance and it paid off. Happens a lot with you." Her arms squeeze me tightly.

"Mmmm." I lean forward to kiss her soft lips. "Not always."

I'm not trying to kill the vibe, but I want her to notice I'm owning up to all the shit I've put her through over the years. No one has tugged her back and forth more than me. I'm aware she's put up with more than anyone should, but I'm so glad she has, because even though I don't deserve her, I still maintain nobody is capable of loving her more than I am.

She leans back, her face serious. "Why are you sharing this all of a sudden? What's changed?"

"Me. I'm sick of carrying this burden alone. I can't do it anymore and there's no one I trust more than you. Plus, I know how badly you've wanted me to open up. Figured I'd start tonight and see how it goes."

"You know you can tell me anything and your secrets will be safe, right?"

I flex my fingers into her hips. "I know. But now do you see why I've been so reluctant to share all this?"

"I do," she acknowledges. "But I'm glad you did. It helps me understand you better. Certain things make more sense now."

"Such as?"

"Why you are the way you are. I've always known about your abandonment issues, but I never really understood the self-destruction and the obsessive need to distract yourself with anything and everything. It helps keep the darkness at bay, doesn't it?"

I nod.

Her fingertips slide through my disheveled hair. "Am I a distraction? A temporary filler for a void?"

"You're much more than that," I assure her. "But you've been used for that purpose, yes."

"Sexually?"

"Yes."

Her face falls with disappointment.

"Aye," I tilt her chin up. "You have to bear with me. I'm not good at this stuff. You're not going to like every answer that comes out of my mouth, but my honesty has to count for something, right? Otherwise, this is all for nothing."

"Fine. But it doesn't mean I have to like it."

"Fair enough. As long as we're on the same page."

She throws her hands up, exasperated. "When are we ever on the same page?"

I crack a small smile despite the heavy subject matter. Leave it to Raven to help me find the positive in something, no matter how bleak it may appear. Her fierce hope against all odds is what makes her both inspiring and delusional.

"There've been some bumps in the road," I admit.

"Bumps? Try potholes."

"Okay, so our track record isn't the greatest, but I'd like to think we're not completely shit out of luck."

"As I recall, you once told me that it would happen for us one day. Funny how that seems so close, yet so far away."

A wave of guilt washes over me. I swallow it down and slip my hands under the hem of her shirt, softly running my fingers up her bare back. The skin-to-skin contact is mollifying. Helps me formulate what I want to say.

"I want to do this right, but I'm afraid of failing you. You've been the one consistent person in my life for seven years. I know I've hurt you in the past, but you've managed to forgive me. Probably because of the friendship. I'd be lying if I said I wasn't concerned about losing that luxury. You may not tolerate as much bullshit once we're in a relationship, and knowing me, I'll find a way to fuck it all up. I always do."

"So we'll take it slow and see how it goes," she proposes. "I can modify my expectations a little bit if you're willing to put forth effort on your part. It's the perfect compromise."

"And if I can't meet your expectations?"

She exhales. "Then we revert back to old patterns and die a pathetic pair of lonely, miserable, tragic lovers."

"Now *that's* romance."

"Shakespeare would approve."

"Just don't kill yourself, okay? I know you're dramatic by nature, but that's going a tad overboard."

She tilts my face up and kisses me senseless. I groan my appreciation and press her chest against mine. In an ideal world, I'd never have to let go of this feeling.

"Does this mean we're in a relationship?" she asks, breaking the kiss.

"This means we're trial and error. If the product works, we'll slap a label on it."

"I can live with that as long as you promise to ditch the latte girls."

My brows shoot up. "The what?"

"Your side chicks. I like to call them latte girls."

"Do you now?" I couldn't hide my amusement even if I tried. She nods.

"Consider it done."

"Good. Now let's take this back to my place," she suggests.

No argument here.

The sound of a camera shutter goes off as Raven snaps photo after candid photo of me absorbed in a graffiti mural. Ever since my spiel last week about not having enough memorable experiences to document, she's taken it upon herself to provide me with an abundance of them. We've banked a disgusting number of Kardashian-worthy selfies, along with scenic snapshots from our nature walks. Who knew isolation with my dream girl could be so relaxing? Normally, my mind wouldn't be able to handle the lack of distractions, but I'm adjusting to this whole self-discovery thing better than I expected. Raven, on the other hand, is whining nonstop about the bugs.

"Seriously, do I have a sign on my forehead that says 'Eat me'?"

I stop spraying, turn around, and raise an eyebrow.

She purses her lips. "You know what I mean."

The corners of my mouth lift into a grin. I resume painting.

We're hanging out at the HOPE Outdoor Gallery where artists can come and graffiti freely without having to worry about getting arrested or fined. It's a safe place where our work can be appreciated instead of ridiculed. I do miss the thrill that comes with the illegal stuff, but it's not worth the risk anymore. Not when there's an option like this available.

After putting the finishing touches on my most recent contribution for society, I take a step back to admire the results. A giant blue teddy bear graces the center of the wall—a cigar in one hand, a pale pink shotgun in the other. A red banner falls from above with the words "Suicide is for Quitters" plastered across it. I'm all about promoting positive messages.

Hypocrisy at its finest.

Raven captures a few pics, knowing it'll be gone in a couple days when another artist comes along and paints over it.

Out with the old, in with the new.

"Are you hungry?" she asks in between snaps.

"Starving."

"Me too. Wanna meet up with Chase and Mia to grab some Tex-Mex?"

I walk over, cup her chin, and bring her in for a swift kiss. "Sounds good, baby."

"I'll meet you in the car."

I load up all my paint cans and follow her down. I'm amazed at how well things are going. I know it's only the early stages, but I was expecting all sorts of drama to rise up and defeat us before we even had a chance to succeed. Always does. It's different this time, though, which makes me nervous. I'm still waiting for the other shoe to drop. I don't want us to fall apart, but history shows a long-standing relationship isn't promising. Maybe we got it right this time. Or maybe I'm just doing what I've always done every time something good happens in my life—mentally preparing for its inevitable demise.

We hit up Freebirds for some burritos and chips 'n' queso. As soon as we walk in, Chase and Mia stand up and join us in the order line. Chase and I pay, then we all grab a table and tear into our food.

A few bites in, Chase starts throwing curious glances between Raven and me. "So, are y'all a thing now?"

"Something like that," I reply, dunking a chip in queso and popping it in my mouth.

"Yeah, but he won't give me the label," Raven gripes.

Chase looks at me like I'm an idiot. "You won't give her the label?"

"We're taking it slow. Besides, everyone knows my heart belongs to you," I bat my eyes at him.

Mia laughs and Raven chokes on her rice.

Unamused, Chase refuses to let the subject drop.

"After all these years, you still won't budge?"

Mia leans forward in her chair. "Whoa, whoa, wait. What do you mean 'after all these years'?" She cuts her gaze to Raven. "You told me you've only liked Eric for the last year."

"It's complicated," she dismisses.

I freeze with my drink near my lips. *Why would Raven tell Mia she's only been into me for a year? Is she ashamed of her feelings for me or something?*

"Unbelievable," Mia leans back, irked. "Not only am I the last to know everything, but I'm deliberately served bullshit."

"You and me both," I mutter, raising my glass in the air.

Raven ignores my comment and sips on her sweet tea. No doubt I'll be hearing about this later. Probably somewhere in the ballpark of thirty times.

Chase clears his throat. "Anyway…"

"Enough about us. What about you two?" I ask, all too eager to shine the spotlight on someone else.

Mia perks up and locks eyes with Chase. I'm sincerely hoping Raven and I don't look this sappy in public.

"Same as you guys. Taking things slow," she answers.

"What's your definition of slow? 'Cause this," I motion between the two of them, "is moving faster than a bad case of the Taco Bell shits."

Mia scrunches up her nose. "That's disgusting."

"Ew, Eric. We're eating here," Raven complains.

Chase laughs and gives me a knowing look.

"We're doing what works for us. There. How about that?" Mia sasses.

I slap my palms down on the table and stiffen. "Hold up. You mean to tell me that people can take their relationships at whatever pace they desire? No conventional methods necessary?" I turn to seize Raven's face in my hands and give her a hard shake. "My God, Rave. What have we done? Did we miss the memo?"

Mia kicks me under the table. "All right. You made your point."

I release Raven and settle back into my chair with a triumphant smirk.

Mia frowns.

"Don't look so offended, Strawberry. Rave and I, we've been on training wheels for years. Can't seem to get off the damn things. It's relationships for retards and I'm the biggest one. I haven't even taken her out on a real date yet."

I pause and process those last words. *Way to miss the mark, Eric.*

As if I didn't feel undeserving of her already, now I've sunk to a new level of humiliation. The single most important person in my life has been settling for mediocre romance. WTF is wrong with me?

The rest of the group falls back into a familiar rhythm of laughter and sarcastic banter, while I'm off in my own world desperately trying to figure out a way to rectify the situation.

FOURTEEN

r a v e n

"Turn around and let me get a good look at you."

I spin and face my laptop screen so Tori can check out my outfit. I've chosen a floral sundress that flares out at the hips and rose pink pumps, forgoing my usual assortment of accessories and over-the-top makeup. I wanted to change it up for a more natural look and take Eric by surprise for our date. He's always telling me to keep it real in all forms.

"Do you think he'll like it?" I ask timidly, smoothing out non-existent wrinkles in my skirt.

"Definitely. And can I just say how stoked I am that y'all have finally pulled your heads out of your asses?"

"You and me both."

"Where's he taking you?"

"No idea. It's supposed to be a surprise."

She grins. "Even better."

A loud knock on my front door cuts our Skype session short.

"That's him. Gotta go," I say, wrestling my feet into my pumps and rushing to the other side of the room for one final glance in the mirror.

"Okay. Have fun tonight. Call or text me when you get home and tell me everything."

"Will do," I assure.

"Bye!"

"Bye!"

The call ends. I exhale, seize my clutch, and try to be casual. "Come in."

Eric lets himself in. I slow my pace in the middle of the hallway, anxiously awaiting his reaction. He closes the door and turns to face me. His eyes widen. A slow smile appears as his eyes rake my body from head to toe.

"Do we really have to leave this apartment right now?"

"Yes."

His shoulders sink. He strides over, tilts my chin up, brings me in for a series of chaste kisses.

"Hate it when you ruin my fun," he says.

"Get used to it."

He releases my chin and digs through a bag I didn't even realize he was holding.

"What's in there?"

He swings it away from my prying eyes.

"None of your business. Is Mia home?"

"No, she's job hunting. Why? You wanna take her out instead?"

"Very cute."

I smile. "I try."

He glances at the clock on the microwave.

"Shit. We gotta bounce or we're gonna be late. Come on."

Eric drives like a maniac until we reach our destination. He cruises into a parking lot filled with cars, finds a spot somewhere in the middle. He parks, cracks the windows, and kills the engine. A large movie screen graces the lot next to a couple of food trucks. The sun's just beginning to set.

"Ever been to a drive-in?" Eric asks.

I shake my head, feeling very out of place with my dress and heels on.

"They're the best," he insists.

"I'm way overdressed. Why didn't you tell me to change?"

"We didn't have time. You take forever to get ready as it is. Besides, I'm a fan of the outfit," he gently tugs on the hem of my dress and gives me a crooked smile.

He reaches into the back seat and grabs the reusable bag I saw him carrying earlier. He pulls out two plastic forks, two plastic cups, and a variety of different desserts, placing them all on the dash. Everything from molten chocolate cake to strawberry cheesecake to tiramisu greets my eyes. My stomach growls in response.

"Picked these up from H-E-B on the way over. Thought you might be hungry."

Oh, my God. Pretty sure I just fell in love with him all over again. Of course, in true Eric fashion, he also pulls out a large bottle of wine.

"We can't drink that in here," I tell him.

"Says who?"

I give him my no-nonsense stare. "Eric, if we get caught we're screwed. We're in a car for crying out loud."

"Relax. It's just one glass. You'll be the one doing most of the work. You know wine is not my preference."

"There are people all around us."

"So we'll wait until it gets dark," he says with an obvious tone.

He sticks the bottle down between his legs and peels off the foil seal from around the neck.

I glance around nonchalantly to make sure no one is watching. Thankfully, everyone's absorbed in their own conversations.

"Do you have a wine opener?"

"Sure do."

He reaches over, pops the glove box open, grabs a paintbrush. He uses the sharp end to press down on the cork with all his might.

"You look constipated."

"It's a good look on me, right?"

I stifle a grin.

He presses down again, his face turning as bright red as the sunset. He exhales harshly. "Hold the bottle, dude."

I double over and hold the bottle still while he concentrates on whittling the cork down. We're starting to draw attention, making me paranoid. With a squeaky *pop,* the cork shoots straight down into the bottle. I sit up and immediately glance around to find everything exactly as it was. Eric throws the paintbrush back into the glove compartment and relaxes.

"Damn, they really make you work for it."

"Not so easy when you don't have a proper opener, is it?"

He doesn't answer. Instead, he cradles the bottle between his feet and waits for the sun to fully set before pouring me a glass.

"How often do you come here?" I ask.

"Probably three or four times a year. I figured since we both love movies and it's become tradition for me, I'd bring you. The vibe is spot-on. Beautiful sunset, breathtaking girl, classy desserts, rundown parking lot, sketchy neighborhood, cork-filled wine, plastic utensils: It's urban meets upscale." He looks over and smiles. "Just like us."

"Why do you insist on believing you're unrefined? You're not."

"I am when I'm sitting next to you," he argues.

"Whatever. I've never treated you that way."

"I know. That's what I love about you."

I swallow past the lump in my throat. That's the closest he's ever come to dropping the "L" word. Since he's not one to express vulnerability more than once in a near decade, I hold on tight to the feeling.

As if on cue, our attention is summoned to the screen when the opening credits for *The Breakfast Club* start rolling. I squeeze his hand and shift around in my seat, unable to contain my excitement. Thank God it's not a stoner comedy. With Eric, you never know what you're in for. Could've been something stupid like *Pineapple Express.*

"It's eighties night," he explains.

"You're the best boyfriend ever."

My body tenses.

Nooooo!

Must fabricate an explanation before he freaks out.

"Uh, I mean—"

He silences me with a reassuring kiss.

"Shh. No talking during the movie," he whispers against my lips.

He sits back and stares at the screen without a care in the world, as if I didn't just drop one of the most frightening words for a commitment phobe. Only word worse than *boyfriend* is *exclusivity*. Of course, I could have called him the old ball and chain. That little gem signals imminent death in the eyes of tools everywhere. *See, Rave? It could've been worse.*

I reach out and not-so-secretly slide the tiramisu off the dash until it magically falls into my lap. Would you look at that! I peek over at Eric, then back down at the dessert. Eyes on Eric. Eyes on yummy dessert. Finally, he sighs and says, "Just grab a fork and eat it, Raven."

Well, if he insists....

I snag one of the plastic forks sitting in the cup holder and dig in. Tastes like heaven. He grabs the other fork and tears into the chocolate cake. I lean over and steal a bite. Or three. Before long, we're both completely engrossed in the movie. Then we're engrossed in a heavy make-out sesh. I blame Molly Ringwald and Judd Nelson. They started it. Cliché? Yup. Do I care? Nope. I'm a Princess and he's a Criminal. Sound familiar?

FIFTEEN

e r i c

I park the car with a weighted heart and even heavier conscience. It's that time again. I've put off visiting my mom for far too long. Miraculously, she's been in the same spot for the last six months.

Never fucking happens.

I glance down at my hand to make sure I'm in front of the same address I've written down. Ladies and gentlemen, we have a match. I kill the engine and brace myself for the familiar shitstorm that's brewing. Old habits die hard.

I slip my sunglasses into the collar of my shirt and knock on the door, eager to get this over with. A few seconds later, it opens up to reveal a shirtless, tattooed, middle-aged man with long greasy hair.

Mom and her wannabe rockers....

"Can I help you?" he asks, sizing me up.

"I'm looking for Holly. Is she here?"

"And you are?"

"None of your concern."

Over his shoulder, I recognize my mom's favorite old scrapbook displayed proudly on the end table. It's filled with all her favorite childhood memories—ones that are "pre-me." That's all the confirmation I need. Rugged Fabio starts to shut the door when I notice the gold wedding band on his finger. Mom's not married. *Fantastic.* What a piece of shit. I stick my foot in the door and push my way through.

"What do you think you're doing?"

I ignore him and search the apartment. "Mom?"

My mom stumbles out of the bedroom wearing what I'm assuming is Fabio's T-shirt. She's sans pants. She tucks a loose strand of blonde hair behind her ear. A brief moment of surprise registers. It's instantly replaced with anger. She attempts to cover her bare legs.

"Eric, what are you doing here? I told you to call first."

"Nice to see you too, Mom. How's life treating you?"

"Don't be a smartass," she snaps, backtracking to fetch a pair of shorts off the floor. She turns her attention to the wannabe rocker. "Mark, this is my son, Eric. Eric, this is Mark. He's a good friend."

"Clearly," I deduce.

Reluctantly, he steps forward and offers his hand. I don't bother to shake it.

"Don't be rude," my mom scolds.

I point over my shoulder. "Don't you think his wife would find it rude that you're fucking each other behind her back?"

"Watch it," she warns.

"Don't talk to your mother that way. What's going on between us is none of your business," Mark adds.

I laugh at their blatant lack of credibility. My hands leisurely run through my hair before I turn back to the woman who was forced to give birth to me. I've been here all of two seconds (which is one second too many) and I'm over it.

"You know, I actually came here to have a real conversation with you. I wanted to see how you're doing and share what's new in my life. Explain how I'm dating a girl I'm crazy about, how I'm considering going back to school and switching jobs, how my art continuously keeps getting better and better. But you don't care about any of that, do you?"

Too much emotion. I pull a Mia and slip my sunglasses over my eyes to shield myself from her disarming stare. My mom and I don't talk about this shit. Ever.

I give her a reasonable five seconds to respond, but she comes up short. What else is new? We always seem to fail each other on every count—except one. Handing me off to my uncle was arguably the best thing she's ever done for both our sakes, even though I hated her for it at the time.

"What a waste of a trip," I mutter, heading for the door.

"Eric, wait," she pleads.

I stop.

She looks torn but doesn't say anything more.

"For the record, I didn't ask for this shit to happen to me any more than you did. Keep that in mind the next time you want to blame me for all your problems."

That one penetrates her I-don't-give-a-fuck exterior. She actually has the decency to look hurt. It doesn't last, though. Never does. Her face flushes with shame when her eyes meet Mark's. Oh, darn. Looks like she has some explaining to do.

I slam the door and manage to avoid letting it hit my ass on the way out. The blinding sun hits my face like a spotlight, exposing my discomfort. Already one step ahead with these shades on. No wonder Mia uses this tactic—works like a charm.

Even though I did my part, I feel incomplete. Closure is a luxury many people don't even realize they have. Going through life in a perpetual state of disconnect is exhausting. And aggravating. What's worse, your closure is often tied to another person. Problematic when they don't feel like cooperating. Thank you, Mom, for not only making my life ten times harder than it had to be, but for refusing to validate my pain on top of that.

SIXTEEN

r a v e n

Finals are right around the corner. I've been studying nonstop and busting my butt to finish up my internship hours. After pouring my third cup of coffee, I carefully review my PowerPoint slides for the umpteenth time. Eric's been helping me study here and there, but his main jobs are to keep me caffeinated, sexually sated, and stocked up on highlighters/notecards. He's only excelling in one area. I'll let you guess which one.

Speaking of the devil, in walks Eric with a giant bag of Kerbey Lane in his hand. My schedule's been too hectic for date nights recently, so tonight we've carved out some much-needed alone time. I've been looking forward to it all week.

"Breakfast for dinner. Is there anything better?" he asks rhetorically.

"What'd you order?"

He sets the bag down on the counter and pulls out two Styrofoam containers.

"Apple-cinnamon pancakes with bacon and scrambled eggs, and biscuits 'n gravy with sausage links and fresh fruit. Which one are you feelin'?"

"Pancakes, please."

"Thought so," he says, checking the containers to see which one is which.

He steals two forks from the kitchen drawer and plops down beside me on the couch. The last couple months have been a relatively smooth ride. We're working through our issues and insecurities. Opening up is becoming more routine for him but curbing my jealousy and trusting him not to screw me over has proven to be a recurring challenge. Sometimes I win that battle, sometimes I don't. Most importantly, Eric's starting to recognize his own worth. I just hope he can sustain it.

"How was work?" I ask.

"Long."

He takes a bite of biscuit and closes his eyes in utter contentment.

"Mmmm. Damn, that hits the spot."

"Thanks for grabbing food," I tell him.

"My pleasure, baby. Thought you could use a break. How much time do you need to set aside for studying tonight?"

I snarf a bite of pancake and shrug.

"Anything I can do to help?"

I shake my head.

"In that case, I'll probably dip out and hang with Chase after this."

His words hit a nerve. I convince myself I must've heard him wrong and swallow my food. "You just saw him two days ago."

"Yeah. So?"

"Don't you want to spend time with me?"

"Of course I do, but you're busy."

I set my container down on the coffee table and turn to face him. "Are you serious?"

"Why are you getting worked up about this?"

"Because I've hardly seen you these past couple weeks. We don't even have time for Thursday Movie Nights anymore. If I'm not studying, I'm working late at the restaurant, or cramming last-minute hours at the boutique. Then, on the one night we actually have plans to hang out together, you go and make other plans of your own. Shady much?"

"How is your lack of availability my fault?"

"I didn't say it was. But I am asking you stay the night."

As much as he tries to keep it subdued, I don't miss the annoyance that flashes through his eyes.

"What's that look for?"

"I honestly don't see the point in hanging out if you're going to be studying all night, that's all. Seems pointless."

"Eric, how many times have you dragged me to places and events I would never go to on my own? A ton. I do it because I know it's important to you, even if I don't necessarily want to be there. It's called give and take."

"Don't sit there and lecture me on balance. I think I've been a great team player, all things considered."

"Why are you getting so defensive?"

He stands up and runs his hands through his hair. "Because this is ridiculous. I don't want to share you with a million other distractions. If your time and attention are going to be split, I'd rather wait until I can have you all to myself. I don't see the problem with that."

"If we were going by that standard, I'd never see you."

"Again, not my fault. You can't blame me for wanting your full attention."

"And you can't blame me for wanting to see my boyfriend once in a while."

"Maybe we should call it a night and quit while we're ahead."

I slouch back into the couch. "If that's what you want."

"Don't do that," he snaps. "Don't test me after you've deliberately set me up to fail."

"I'm not," I lie.

"The hell you aren't. I know a trap when I see one."

I stand up. "If you want to go, just go! I'm not stopping you."

It's quiet.

Too quiet.

We stare at each other, the space charged with palpable tension. Anger burns in his crystal blue eyes. He bends down to grab his biscuits 'n gravy and strides over to store them in the fridge. A tiny sliver of hope blooms in my chest at the thought that he might be back for them later. Or maybe he's just saving them for me. My heart sinks at that prospect.

He grabs his keys off the counter. "When you cool off, text me."

No promises.

The front door opens and closes. I glance down at my pancakes, no longer feeling hungry. I hate it when he walks out during an argument. Biggest relationship pet peeve. Why do people do that? Quitters.

I huff and get up to put my leftovers in the fridge. I grab a bottle of wine out of the door while I'm at it, forgoing the glass. I pop it open, raise the bottle to my lips, take generous gulps. Drinking when you're pissed is never a good idea, but when there's no one around to bitch at or cry to, I say go for it.

An hour later, I've drained what was left in the bottle. Always a downer when that happens. Too drunk and aggravated to study, I saunter into the bedroom and crawl onto my comfortable bed and allow myself to pass out. Screw the impending hangover.

Sometime during the middle of the night, I'm vaguely aware of the bed shifting. A warm body presses against my back. Paint fumes rouse my senses. Fingers idly stroke my hair. I inhale deeply and moan my appreciation. My heavy eyelids close and I fall back into a peaceful, drunken slumber, but not before a kiss meets my temple and the words "I love you, Rave," are softly whispered into my ear.

There's no happiness in his words.

Only sadness and defeat.

A reaction I attribute to our fight.

Eric

I've been seeing a therapist for the last few weeks. Raven has no idea. Not because she's against therapy, but because she'd freak out if she knew the real reason why I'm sitting on this couch. In her mind, everything's starry eyes and fairy tale finales. Truth is, I'm slipping. The delicate façade I've created to keep her happy is crumbling, and I can't glue the pieces back together fast enough.

If she only knew how much I desperately want to hit the self-destruct button, just so I can end the constant fear of letting her down. It haunts me every day. The anxiety is crippling. How do people deal? I'm not sure how much longer I can continue on like this. It's exhausting pretending to be happy when I'm not. The amount of energy it takes to forge a smile is becoming unmanageable—hence my being here.

"You seem on edge," Dr. Coleman observes.

No shit, Doc. Now fix me.

"I can't sleep. The stress of my anxiety is keeping me up at night."

"Do you know what's causing it?"

I shake my head. "It seems to be pouring out of everywhere."

"How often are you experiencing these feelings?"

"Depends. At least a couple times a day. Usually more."

"And on a scale from one to ten, ten being the worst, how bad would you say the symptoms are?"

I shrug. "I don't know. Seven?"

He jots that down. "Walk me through what's bothering you."

"Where do I even begin?"

"Wherever you want," he encourages.

My sweaty palms rub up and down my thighs nervously. No matter how many times I go through this process, I never seem to get acquainted with it.

I exhale and flush my thoughts out in one shaky breath before I have a chance to reconsider.

"I feel like I have no idea where I'm going in life. I'm completely lost. I have no concept of what I want to do; no real grasp on who

I am, which is terrifying. It doesn't help that failure is always in the back of my mind. Especially in regard to my current relationship, so I hold back to avoid disappointing anyone. This has been the norm throughout my life, by the way."

"The fear of failure? Or holding back?"

"Both." I clarify.

"Okay. Keep going," he urges, sensing there's more.

"I think people's expectations are daunting and unfair. No matter how hard I try, I don't live up to the standard that's been set. I hate settling for mediocrity in any sense, but I don't feel I deserve any better. I'm also afraid my mom will never forgive me for ruining her life, even though I didn't do anything wrong. But most of all, I'm scared shitless because deep down I know that one way or another, I'll probably have to break up with Raven in order to fix this mess. She'll never want anything to do with me again. And not only will I have lost my best friend in the entire world, but I'll have lost the one person who believes in me the most. It's unbearable. So I disguise my true feelings and keep trudging on."

Gulp. Well, there you have it.

"Are you in love with her?" he asks.

"Easily. And if I'd waited to pursue something with her until I got my shit together, this wouldn't even be an issue. But I've already fucked up one too many times. She's fresh out of free passes, and I need like ten more."

Hindsight blows.

"Let's back up for a minute. Tell me what you meant when you said the part about ruining your mother's life. What happened there?"

I proceed to tell him everything—the bad, the ugly, and the really fuckin' ugly. He listens attentively, absorbing all I have to say.

I keep it 100, even though part of me is dying to hold something back for my own preservation. I'm wise enough now to know that if I'm not open and brutally honest, it'll get me nowhere. And I want to be better. Not only for Raven, but for myself. If there's one thing she's taught me, it's that effort is everything. What you put into this world is what you get out of it. So I'm gonna give this all I got and pray it's enough.

"Have you ever tried talking to your mom about what you've both been through?"

"No. That would be too functional for my family's standards."

"Do you think she'd be willing to listen to what you have to say?"

"Probably not," I answer truthfully. "She's been running from her pain for as long as I can remember. Besides, I'm not interested in repairing the relationship with my mom. I'm much more concerned about saving the relationship with my girlfriend."

Doc nods. "I understand where you're coming from. But as your therapist, I'm more concerned about the relationship with your mom. Many of your unresolved issues stem from your childhood. If the two of you can sit down and manage an honest conversation, there's a good chance you'll be able to start working through some of these obstacles. Otherwise, you're both bound to keep repeating the same patterns over and over again—including in your relationships."

"And if she shuts me down? Then what?"

"Then you and I focus on moving forward regardless."

"So you're telling me I can swing this whole happy and healed thing without her?"

"Of course you can. I just don't want to rule out the possibility of a relationship with your mom if there's still one in the cards."

"There's not."

"Consider giving it a shot."

I open my mouth to protest.

He raises a hand and cuts me off. "You don't have to do anything right now, but keep it in the back of your mind for later. We'll talk about it the next time I see you."

I rest my back into the couch and exhale my relief.

I can do this, I tell myself.

For the first time in years, there's a glimmer of light at the end of the tunnel. Raven's face appears in my mind. Then, like a gust of wind extinguishing an open flame, that flicker of light vanishes. A wave of dread washes over me. I swallow my unease and look back up.

"What do I do about Raven? I can't let her down again. There's gotta be a way to work through this and still maintain a relationship with her, right?"

"It's your call. Is the relationship toxic?"

"It's the healthiest one I've ever had."

"You're not dependent on her?"

I tiptoe around the truth. "Not excessively. I'm an abandonment kid, remember? I push everyone away."

"Unless you've grown accustomed to having her in your life. In which case, you might be latching onto her *because* of your history with abandonment."

"We're good," I assure, all cool and collected.

No, really. Everything's fine.

We're going to pull through this.

That's my story and I'm sticking to it.

SEVENTEEN

r a v e n

Holidays came and went. Winter passed by in a blur. My final semester kicked off with a wild bash and ended with a full-blown graduation extravaganza. Despite all these back-to-back surreal events, one thing has become achingly clear—Eric's detachment from me. I've been watching him gradually slip away, drifting quietly in the midst of all the noise. He doesn't even tell me where he goes anymore. We've fallen into a well-versed routine where I ask what's bothering him, and he responds with a stoic, "Nothing, I'm fine." Not wanting to be the pushy girlfriend, I drop the subject and wait until the next day rolls around to express my concern. He's anything but fine. Even something as simple as going through the motions seems too much for him to bear.

My bed no longer smells like him because he no longer smells like him. The paint fumes are absent. He kisses me and it's empty and fraudulent. Just like his smiles. And his conversations. And our relationship. Who is this shell of a person? My heart is in the hands of a stranger. *Maybe he can still rally,* I hopelessly tell myself. *Maybe if I love him enough for the both of us, he'll come back around.* But that never really works, does it?

I'd trade anything to have the old Eric back. But more than that, I'd give anything to see him happy again. The pain of watching him suffer in silence is worse than admitting to myself that our relationship is over. We're too far gone. I guess that's why I'm not overly surprised to walk in the door and find him standing in the middle of my living room with a black duffel bag resting at his feet, a tortured expression on his face.

It's the first sign of genuine emotion he's shown in months.

My stomach drops. I swallow and push the door shut behind me, bracing myself for the impending storm. I shrug my jacket off and toss it onto the couch, then cross my arms over my chest protectively and motion my head toward the bag.

"What's that for?" I ask, already knowing the answer.

He rubs the back of his neck and lifts his gaze to mine. The depth of remorse in his eyes completely guts me. Makes the silence even more excruciating. He clenches his jaw. "I'm sorry."

I stare at the ground and dig my heel into the carpet. It takes every ounce of strength I have not to break down in front of him. I make myself focus on keeping my voice even and my heart steady. Both are futile.

"Where are you going?"

"I need to get out here for a while. Find out what I want to do with my life and actually make something of myself."

"When are you coming back?"

He shifts back and forth uncomfortably.

"I'm not sure. I just need some time to figure things out. Hanging around here isn't helping my situation."

A jolt of panic runs through me. What if he doesn't come back? What if I never see him again? And what does he mean by here? My apartment? Austin? Texas as a whole? I know his words aren't directed at me, but his tone suggests I'm part of the problem.

"What about your job?"

"Today was my last day."

My head snaps up. This isn't a spur of the moment decision. He's been planning this trip for a while. Probably longer than I realize. Why didn't he say anything?

A stream of silent tears fall down my face. "Why didn't you tell me you were so unhappy? We could've figured this out."

"No, we couldn't. This is something I need to do on my own."

I shake my head vehemently, not accepting that answer. He steps forward to comfort me.

I take a considerable step back. "Don't," I warn. "You don't get to be the good guy in this scenario."

His shoulders sink. "Rave, this has nothing to do with you. This is on me. Please try to understand."

"Understand what, exactly? That you're leaving me? That instead of confiding in me, you chose to shut me out like you always have? You didn't even try, Eric. The one thing I asked of you, and you couldn't follow through."

He holds his hands out, trying to reason with me. "What would I have said? That I'm fucking miserable? That I have no clue where my life is heading? I didn't have any answers for you. I still don't have any answers."

I use the backs of my fists to wipe the tears from my eyes. All it does is make room for new ones. "It's not about having the answers. I understand not knowing what you want. I understand feeling scared because you have no idea what comes next. God, I can even relate to the overwhelming desire to leave and go find yourself. I'm all for that. What I don't get is why you didn't have the decency to tell me this months ago? I must've asked you a thousand times what was wrong, and you never once said a word."

He doesn't say anything. He can't because he knows I'm right. Whether he meant to or not, he screwed me over. *Again.* And I'm left wondering why we ever even dared to step out of the friend zone.

"Please don't look at me like that," he begs.

"Like what?"

"Like I'm a traitor. You have no idea how much this is killing me. I've tried so hard to make this work. I wanted to avoid hurting you at all costs, but I couldn't hold on any longer."

"So you strung me along out of fear and pity? Gee, when you put it that way, getting dumped doesn't seem so bad," I snap.

"It was never going to work and you know it. I've been sinking like an anchor and dragging you down with me. You didn't sign up for a lifetime of playing fixer upper. It was only a matter of time before you started resenting me."

"I resent you now!"

He winces at my outburst. I drop my gaze and try to ignore the unsettling feeling rising up in the pit of my stomach. He walks over, cups my face in his hands, and tilts it upward, desperate to get through to me. "For the first time in my life, I'm not running from anything. I'm fully prepared to deal with everything I need to and face it all head-on. Then I'm coming back for you," he vows.

"Don't bother," I say angrily, yanking my face out of his grasp. "Just go."

He backs up, stunned. There's no point in listening anymore. I stare off to the side, not willing to engage in this conversation. Perhaps he'll get a taste of his own medicine.

When he refuses to leave, I yell, "Get out!"

He hesitates for a moment, unsure of what to do next. Ultimately, he succumbs and wraps a hand around the back of my neck, bringing my forehead to his lips. Warm tears dampen my skin. "I love you," he murmurs into my hair, inhaling my scent like he's committing it to memory. "So fucking much."

The gesture makes everything hurt a million times more. I squeeze my eyes shut and try to concentrate on anything but his departing words.

When the door shuts, I wander into my room, crawl across the bed, and collapse, hugging a pillow to my chest like a broken child. Sobs wrack my body for what seems like hours. Somewhere in the midst of all that heartache, I fall into an exhausted sleep.

"Okay, we have Cherry Garcia, Half Baked, and Strawberry Cheesecake. Take your pick," Mia announces, surveying the Ben and Jerry's selection in our freezer.

"Cherry Garcia, please."

"You got it."

She grabs it, along with the Half Baked, and zaps them both in the microwave. She fishes out two giant spoons from the drawer and delivers my fix in record time.

It's been over a week since Eric left. No matter what I do or where I go, everything hurts. All the time. I keep waiting for it to subside long enough so I can pretend to enjoy a glass of wine, but you can't cheat emotional pain. I've experienced heartbreak before, but this is different. Eric was my first everything. No amount of drinking, eating, crying, or venting can undo the mark he's left on my life, let alone my heart. If I could go back in time to the very first moment I met him and give my younger self some advice, I'd just stand there in front of her, looking as atrocious as I do now, and point to young Eric as the culprit.

There. Problem solved.

Now where's my time machine?

Music, rom-coms, and art have all been banned from our apartment. Blonds, black hoodies, blue eyes, '80s movies, stoner comedies, happy couples, and anything relating to James Dean are next to go. The urge to drive to his place and see if his furniture is still there—or if he still is—hits me every day. I could just ask Mia, but that would mean she knows more about his whereabouts than I do, and that's a bitter pill to swallow. Plus, I think it's better for everyone involved if I'm unaware. I need to concentrate on moving forward, not holding out hope that he may return.

"Have you checked the mail to see if any design schools have gotten back to you?" Mia asks.

A couple months back, I sent out numerous applications to art institutes. I've received letters from four, but I'm too scared to open them. Those envelopes hold way too much power. Everything I've worked for hinges on what's revealed inside. Oh, and another tiny detail: zero of the schools are located in Austin.

"Not yet," I lie. "They'll probably come in the next week or so."

"You applied for fall semester, right?"

I scoop a bite of ice cream into my mouth and nod. I watch as she puts two and two together and gives me a dubious look. Surprisingly, she doesn't press the issue. Maybe she figures I'm dealing with enough as it is. Whatever the reason, I'm grateful.

She sets her ice cream down on a coaster and adjusts the hem of her shirt, then kicks her feet up on the couch and gives me her full attention.

"Listen, I know the timing sucks, but I really need to talk to you about something," she confesses.

"Fire away."

"I didn't want to drop this on you last minute, so I'm telling you now. Keep in mind I never meant for it to come right on the heels of you and Eric."

"Okaaaay," I say cautiously. "What's up?"

She exhales an unsteady breath.

"Chase asked me to move in with him."

My face falls.

"What? When?"

"A couple days ago," she says, eyeing me with uncertainty. It's a look that reads Fragile: please handle with care. Have I mentioned it drives me crazy when people approach me with kid gloves? Makes me want to take *my* gloves off and throw down. Sure, my heart's no longer in pristine condition, but that doesn't mean I won't persevere. Diamonds are forever, honey.

After convincing her that I'm not going to freak out, she relaxes and gives me the rundown. "He wants me to move in ASAP. I told him I'd have to give you a heads up and put in my thirty-day notice. The last thing I want to do is put you in a bind, so if that's cutting it too close, just say the word and we'll figure something else out."

I'm silent. On the one hand, I couldn't be more thrilled. Chase is a great guy and she deserves someone who treats her the way he does. But on the other hand, I need my army of girlfriends. They're my lifelines in this cruel battle of love and war. Where lovers fail, friends rise. Without her, I'll be forced to face my reality for what it really is: lonely and depressing.

Despite all that, I can't bring myself to ruin her happy moment. I plaster on a tight smile and lean over to give her a hug.

"If there's anyone who deserves a stable life, it's you, Mia. You've been through hell and back."

She releases me and stares into my eyes with a glimmer of hope. "Does this mean you're okay with it?"

"Under one condition. I get to be the one to decorate your apartment."

"Oh, God. Are you going to go all out like you do during the holidays? Because I gotta tell you, I don't know if I can handle that. Bright colors and forced cheeriness make me want to gouge my eyes out."

"Don't hold back or anything," I state dryly.

The moment I say those words, it dawns on me that Eric would've said something similar if he were here. He'd play off Mia's energy and churn out a speedy rebuttal, chock-full of sarcasm. I press my hand against my chest in an attempt to suppress the familiar ache and refocus my attention on Mia.

"In all seriousness, though, I call dibs on the shopping and decorating. It'll keep me busy. You and Chase can have a tiny say, but ultimately, I make all the decisions."

"Jesus. You're like a bridezilla, but for interior decorating. What would they call that? A designzilla?"

"I prefer the term boss bitch."

She laughs.

"You'd wear that title well."

"And don't you forget it," I say.

Later in the night, as I'm about to crawl under the covers and give myself over to the divine feeling of freshly washed sheets, my attention drifts to the letters piled up on my vanity. I sit up and reach over to grab them. Tossing my hair over my shoulder, I flip over the first envelope. It's from California College of the Arts. I slide my finger under the tab to rip it open and pull the letter out, carefully unfolding it. My heart nearly stops beating when I see the word *accepted*. I stare at the letter for several seconds. Bittersweet tears fill my eyes. Finally, a chance to prove myself and channel all my energies into my life-long passion. I know I have a long way to go and plenty to learn, but it's a start. Even if every other school rejects me, the amount of gratitude I have for making it into one is indescribable. Anything to get away from here.

Impatient, I tear open the rest of the envelopes to find out the verdicts. I've been accepted to the Art Center College of Design in Pasadena, which is my second choice. Rejected from School of the Art Institute of Chicago, my top choice. And rejected from Rhode Island School of Design. I'm still waiting on a response from one more, but the West Coast is looking pretty damn promising.

If only Eric could be here. He'd be ecstatic. I'm tempted to whip out my phone and text him the results, but I refrain. Better to make a clean break than to complicate things all over again. As long as he continues to have a strong presence in my life, I'll always want more. We need separation and distance.

My gaze automatically floats to the painting he made for my eighteenth birthday. That portrait represents every facet of us smashed together in a single canvas. Other than a handful of photos that were too precious to make the burn pile, it's the last piece I have of him. That's the hardest part; wiping all traces of him from my life. I don't know if I can bring myself to get rid of everything. Text messages, voicemails, videos—they all still exist. I'm not using them as torture devices for my heart, but I can't bear to erase them yet. That's a whole 'nother level of saying goodbye.

Why does the one person who I want to share this moment (and all my other moments with) have to be MIA? We would have celebrated a hundred different ways. Managing my pain during the day is one thing, but at night when there are no distractions, and his side of the bed is cold and empty, it's impossible to think about anything else.

EIGHTEEN

eric

"How's the beach?" Dr. Coleman asks.

We're kicking it over Skype.

"Scalding."

Honestly, who complains about being on a beach? Leave it to me to suck the positive out of everything lately. I tack on a pro to avoid sounding like such a whiner. "The water's nice, though."

Doc smiles, noticing what I did there.

Crystal Beach has always been a reliable source for creativity and inspiration but being four-and-a-half hours away from Raven changes things. Somewhere along the way, she became my muse. Then my muse became a constant reminder of my failures, and the well ran dry. Haven't been able to paint or draw since.

Every day I pick up a spray can and stare at a blank canvas, waiting to be inspired. Seconds tick by and turn into minutes, which stretch into hours. Nothing productive ever happens. It's all mind games and wasted time. I'm stuck, in every sense of the word. My coping mechanisms have taken a hiatus. I've had to resort to using other outlets like good ol' Dr. Coleman here to exorcise my bullshit. Goes without saying, he has his work cut out for him.

Just making sure I get my money's worth, that's all.

"How are you feeling today?"

"Better. Still can't break my creative barrier, but mood-wise, I'm doing okay."

"Glad to hear it," he says. "Do you think you'll end up staying there for the entire summer?"

"Haven't decided."

Two years ago, Uncle Max sold his house and bought this place. It's right on the coast, doomed to get swept away by a hurricane, but not today. He's allowing me to stay here for part of the summer while he's on a fishing trip. When I initially pitched the idea, he laughed hysterically and told me to fuck off. But when I explained the situation and told him how serious I was about getting my shit together, he relented.

"How are you holding up without Raven?"

"Fine," I lie.

Telling from the look on his face, he isn't buying anything I'm selling. Why can't therapists be less perceptive? Would it kill them to accept the lie like everybody else? Smile and nod. Those are the rules. How hard is it to play along?

"I miss her," I cave.

"Have you two spoken since you left?"

I shake my head. "What would I say? I'm the reason she's hurting. In her mind, I didn't even try. I'm just the asshole who dumped her and left." I pause and clench my jaw, working it over back and forth. "It's not like I can undo anything or make it better. What's the point in calling?"

"You made the right decision."

I glance up at the screen and shoot him a look of incredulity. This is the first time he's voiced his opinion on the matter. He leans back in his office chair and swivels from side to side.

"When you look back on this, I think you'll be glad you took the time to focus on yourself and confront your issues. I know it must seem like you're going through hell now, but you'll be stronger for it in the end."

"Better be," I mutter. "I've sacrificed too much. I want her back when this is all over."

"Let's take things one step at a time. I don't want you getting ahead of yourself here."

My non-negotiation face appears. "Look, Doc, I refuse to settle on this one. I've settled my whole life. I've spent way too much time absorbed in the wrong people, the wrong activities, and the wrong mindset. Not many risks I've taken have been worth the outcome, but she's different. Smartest decision I've ever made was falling in love with her. I'm going to win her back. I need you to get on board with the plan because it's the one topic that's not up for debate. Anything else is fair game."

"She may not be willing to take you back, Eric. Prepare yourself for that."

And there it is. My deepest, darkest fear materialized. What if this is truly the end for Raven and me? Friends, lovers—all of it.

What if saying goodbye is the last defining moment, the last real impact, we'll ever have on each other's lives?

I'm distracted when my phone lights up and vibrates beside me on the bed. I pick it up and swipe the screen to read the text.

Chase: *Just checking in to make sure you're alive.*

As I'm about to type a response, Dr. Coleman pipes up. "Put down the phone and pay attention. You're wasting valuable time."

I sigh and toss the phone aside, then sit up and concentrate on him.

"Good. Now listen up. Here's what I want you to do; I want you to call your mom and set up a time for the two of you to sit down and have a conversation."

"Do you have any idea how difficult it is to get ahold of that woman?" I ask, almost laughing. "You may as well be asking for Jesus Christ himself."

"I sincerely doubt it's as hard as you're making it out to be. You've gone to great lengths to avoid her. Now I'm holding you to our deal. If she refuses, then we'll readjust. But the effort needs to be made. No excuses."

"Are you going to prescribe me something to get through that encounter?" I half joke.

"Why are you so quick to try and suppress your feelings? Not every emotion is bad. Sadness and pain have their rightful place in the spectrum."

"When you've been dealt the lion's share of both, it's nice to experience something else for a change."

"I'm not referring you to someone for a prescription. You just want to take the easy route, which is an illusion. It's a temporary fix for a deep-seated problem. You and your mom need to hash this out properly."

"But I'm in emotional distress."

"I can see that," he acknowledges. "But it's nothing out of the ordinary given the circumstances. You've self-medicated in the past. Did it ever make your problems go away? For more than a few hours?"

I narrow my gaze. "Fine. You win. I'll call my mom and ask her to meet up. No guarantees, though."

"I'm only asking you to give it a shot. Text me if you get ahold of her and we can set a time for our next session and discuss it."

"Can't wait," I respond sarcastically.

"Eric?"

I glance at him, fully prepared to be chastised.

"Great job today. I'm proud of you."

His words create a deep, rippling impact. I blink a few times. My lungs deflate, completely caught off guard. I can't remember the last time anyone said that to me. It's comforting to hear I'm doing something right. Especially when I'm putting all this effort in.

"Hang in there, okay? Keep me posted if you decide to come back early so we can meet in person," he says.

"Will do. Thanks for not giving up on me."

"Thanks for not giving up on yourself. Until next time."

"Later."

I end the call and close my laptop. With a light toss, it lands on the foot of the bed. I slip my hands behind my head and lie back to stare up at the ceiling. It's so quiet here. Nothing but waves and birds and chill vibes for miles. Gives me ample time to self-reflect and face all of my issues, which is exactly what I came here for.

Remembering Chase's text, I roll over to the side and grab my phone to reply.

Me: *Yeah. All good. Thanks for asking. How's everything back home?*

I'm assuming he knows what I'm getting at.

Chase: *Same old. We all miss you.*

Me: *How are my girls?*

It takes him a few minutes to respond.

Chase: *One is currently moving in with me, and the other is moving to Cali in a month. She got accepted to a couple design schools out there. We're all throwing her a surprise farewell party at Bellotti's next Friday night. Just in case you want to show up...*

My stomach plummets. I sit up straight and swing my legs to the floor. She's leaving? In a month? That's not enough time. Was she ever planning on telling me?

Me: *Which schools did she get into?*

Chase: *No idea. Sorry, dude. I'm not much help.*

Me: *Do me a favor and find out. That's a big deal.*

Chase: *I'm on it.*

Me: *Congrats on convincing Mia to move in with you, btw. She clearly doesn't know what she signed up for.*

First real joke I've cracked in months.

Chase: *Come back here and tell her that yourself.*

Me: *Nice try. Too soon. Nothing's changed.*

I switch over to my contacts list and pull up Raven's number. For several minutes, I go back and forth on whether or not to push the call button and congratulate her. She's worked so hard for this and it's too important for me to skip out on. Then again, she didn't tell me anything. If she wanted me to know, she would've told me the news herself. I don't want to infringe on her happiness. I've done that enough over the last few months. She deserves to bask in this moment.

Even though it goes against everything in my nature, I press the back button and force myself to search for my mom, instead. I dial what I'm guessing is still her number, raise the phone to my ear, and dread the next however many seconds of uncertainty. On the fourth ring, she picks up.

"Hello?"

"Mom?"

Rustling noises ensue.

"Eric? Is that you?"

Several beats of silence pass before I answer.

"Yeah. Listen, I need a favor. It's important."

"What's going on?"

"We need to have a conversation. In person."

"Why? Did something happen? Are you okay?"

I'm momentarily stupefied by her concern. Did she just feign interest in my well-being? Unprovoked? My bullshit meter is exploding. Must discover her angle and stay two steps ahead.

I wipe the beads of sweat from my forehead and rub my palm up and down my thigh, trying to formulate what I want to say. It'd be much easier if she hadn't just thrown a massive curveball.

"I've been seeing a therapist lately. He wants us to sit down and talk through our issues. All of them. Including, you know...the forbidden ones."

Jesus, I can't even say it out loud. How the hell am I going to sit down and talk about it in person?

She exhales slowly, revealing a sense of unease.

My knee begins to bounce up and down restlessly. I'm terrified she'll say no. I'm even more terrified she'll say yes. *Doc should've referred me to a psychiatrist,* I repeatedly tell myself.

"Where and when do you want to meet up?"

I pause and look down at the phone to make sure I dialed the right number. Who is this woman and what has she done with my mother? I'm careful not to get my hopes up because she's notorious for committing then flaking. I'm proof of that.

"Where are you living?"

"Same place I was last time you visited and stormed out."

Bingo! There's my guilt-tripping mom.

"I'm at Uncle Max's place on the coast. Wanna come here? He's on a fishing trip, so it's just me. I can text you the address."

I'm positive she'll say no, which is all part of my master plan. That way I can get out of the conversation and still tell Doc I tried my best without hearing any flak.

Cunning, but not dishonest.

"Sure, I'll drive down. A trip to the beach sounds nice. I'll have to take time off work, though, so you need to give me a specific time frame."

Goddammit, Mom! The one time I desperately need her to fail me, and she comes through—Mother of the Fucking Year. Am I being Punk'd?

"Uh…"

I can hear her smile on the other end of the line. "Were you counting on me to say no or something?"

I choose not to acknowledge that question.

"How about next Saturday? Does that work?"

"I'll be there."

Now I have a legitimate reason not to go back to Austin for Raven's going away party. It's better this way. If I didn't have an excuse to stay away, I'd probably show up uninvited and end up pissing her off at her own event. Nobody wants me to be that guy.

I exhale harshly. "Alrighty, then. Next Saturday it is."

"Don't sound so excited."

"Mom, let's keep it real. Are you on drugs right now?"

She ignores the question. "I'll see you Saturday, Eric. Text me the address. The *correct* one."

I roll my eyes and fight off mental musings of my suicide. This is what I get for allowing a one-way door to stay cracked open all these years. Should've figured she'd barge her way back through at some point.

We say our goodbyes and hang up. I waste no time forwarding the address. At least she didn't say the words "I love you." How fucking awkward would that have been? I have to keep reminding myself why I'm doing all this. Otherwise, it feels like the world's biggest trap. This is for my younger self, my present self, and my future self. All three deserve to be healed.

Less than a month left to pull my shit together and return to Raven's side before she catches a one-way flight to Cali. I can't let her leave knowing we're on rocky terms. I've gotta make it right, especially if it's my last chance to see her.

NINETEEN

r a v e n

My apartment has never felt more barren. Between Eric leaving and Mia moving out, nothing's familiar. It's all random fragments of a life I used to know. Change is necessary. Transitions are inevitable. That part I was prepared for. But what I didn't expect was an imposter to swoop in and take over the place. She goes by the name Deafening Silence, and she's everywhere, all the time.

It still hasn't sunk in that I'm leaving. I keep waiting to second-guess my decision, but Pasadena is where my heart belongs. It's the one area of my life that still makes sense. Packing has become therapeutic. There's something about seeing actual proof of moving forward that gives me a renewed sense of hope. My thirty-day notice is up in a few weeks, but I'll be out of here before then. Thanks to a depleted college fund, the government and I will be tag teaming the hefty bill for design school. I don't mind, though. Makes it feel more like mine and less like someone else's.

I check the clock on the microwave, gauging how much time I have left before I need to finish getting ready. Chase, Mia, and I are all going downtown for a few drinks. I'm not keen on being the third wheel, but it certainly beats hanging out with Deafening Silence all night.

With twenty minutes to spare, I finish wrapping the last of my wine glasses in newspaper and gently place them in the box. My phone vibrates with an incoming text. I swipe my thumb across the screen and glance down.

Mom: *Hi sweetie. Can you swing by the restaurant on your way downtown?*

Me: *Why? My last shift was a couple days ago.*

Mom: *I know, but we forgot to have you sign some paperwork. It's important.*

Of course it is. Unable to say no to my mom, (or any other family member for that matter) I succumb.

Me: *Give me forty-five minutes.*

Mom: *Thank you!*

I waltz into the bathroom and finish straightening my hair. Tonight I've chosen to attack the sleek, low pony look. Slipping into an all-black jumpsuit and matching pumps, I'm sophistication personified. I stare at my appearance in the mirror, searching for confidence, trying to remember what it feels like to be comfortable in my own skin—to be my old self. Something inside me says that girl will never fully resurrect. How could she? With all the changing tides, she's evolving. I keep trying to convince myself trivial things that used to matter, like having a person in my corner, just don't carry the same weight anymore.

I put on a brave face and whip out my phone to text Mia.

Me: *Ready to go whenever you are. Also, can we swing by the restaurant first? My mom needs me to tie up a couple loose ends.*

Mia: *Sure thing, love. On our way now.*

I lock up the apartment and make my way down. When I round on Chase's Mustang, I fling the door open, slide into the backseat, and come face to face with a beaming Mia. That's how I know she feels sorry for me. She's overenthusiastic, and she's riding bitch.

"Mia, get up front where you belong."

She scowls and crawls across my lap to grab the handle and slams the door shut, then leans back and glares. "Get over yourself. I'm sitting next to you because you're moving soon. We only have a finite amount of time left to spend together, and I want to make the most of it."

"Where to, ladies?" Chase interrupts, throwing an arm behind the passenger's seat and glancing between the two of us.

"Bellotti's," Mia answers.

He turns around and shifts the car in reverse, then switches gears and cruises through the gate.

Mia and I spend the bulk of the drive bonding over the perks and pitfalls of living with boys. She only asks me about Eric once, and whether or not I've heard from him, to which I shake my head and stare out the window. I've reached a place where I can talk about him without feeling resentful, but tonight's different. It's another celebration he's not here for. He didn't miss a single one in eight years, and now he's missing heaps of them.

I've come to realize that Eric needs to be divided into two separate categories: the ex-boyfriend, and the best friend. I don't want the ex-boyfriend here; I want my best friend. They're two entirely different people. My best friend sticks around through thick and thin and always has my back. The ex ditches and leaves, smashing my heart into oblivion on his way out. One is my protector; one is my destroyer. Problem is, I love them both.

Never once did I envision my future without him. How could I? There are certain people in this world that you never think you'll have to learn to live without. Eric was one of those people. He intricately wove himself into the fabric of my life, and now he's gone. We only had so many chances to get it right. We missed our shot. I can't tell if that's mercy, or cruelty.

Before I can analyze everything to death, Chase pulls up to the front of Bellotti's and drops Mia and me off at the door. He drives off to find a parking spot. I glance down and proceed to dig through my clutch for my ID. I'm in dire need of a Cosmo.

"This should only take a sec," I tell her.

"No worries. I'll save a seat at the bar and you can wait for Chase out here."

"You're a riot," I mutter, assuming she's joking. The sound of her footsteps fading tells me she's not. My head snaps up. "Hey, get back here! He's your boyfriend, not mine."

She disregards my comment and disappears into the restaurant. Now I'm stuck on non-boyfriend babysitting duty. I glance around the parking lot, keeping an eye out for Chase. No such luck. A family of four makes their way past me, still no Chase. He's a grown man. He can navigate his own damn self around the world.

I slip my clutch under my arm and head inside. The place is buzzing with chatty customers waiting to be seated. I inch past the horde and make a beeline for the bar. Along the way, Emilio comes waltzing out of the kitchen with a tray of food.

"Hey, sis. What are you doing here?"

"Looking for Mom."

"Hold on a sec." He walks over to a nearby booth and sets the tray down on a stand. Once he's done passing out the food, he grabs the tray and returns my way.

"Where's Mom?" I ask.

He points over his shoulder to the party room. "In there."

"Got it. I'll wait at the bar until she's done."

"No need. Just head in there."

"Uh, what about the guests?"

"They're not your typical customers. Here," he winds his arm around mine, "I'll escort you."

"That's really not necessary," I say, my attention split between him and finding Mia. He ignores my protest and tugs me along.

"It's going to be weird without you," he admits.

There's a sadness in his eyes that wasn't there before. I look away and swallow past the lump in my throat. Of all my siblings, Emilio's going to be the hardest one to say goodbye to.

"It still doesn't feel real. I'm just hoping I don't wind up falling flat on my face and embarrassing myself once I get there."

"You won't. This is your time. Seize the opportunity and don't let go because it may not come around again. And promise me you'll keep in touch, okay? I don't want you forgetting about us when you become the next Rachael Ray."

"Rachael Ray isn't a fashion designer, Emilio."

"Then, um, one of those *Full House* kids?"

"Oh, my God. Give it up."

"One of them is a designer, though. Right?"

"*One* of them? Seriously, stop. You're embarrassing yourself. And, of course, I'll keep in touch. Harassing my favorite older brother is part of my job description. Someone needs to keep you in line."

"Whatever you do, don't tell Andre I'm your favorite. And don't forget you said that, either. When all the famous chicks are strutting your clothes down the runway, this guy expects full backstage access. Especially if one of those models is Gigi Hadid. She's smokin' hot."

I burst out laughing. "You're delusional if you think I'll ever get that big, but I appreciate the vote of confidence."

"Hey, you never know. Leave the doubting to all the haters. Your job is to aim high and catapult yourself to the top. Make that money and be about that business. But most of all, be happy. Wouldn't expect anything less from my favorite sister."

"Better not tell Ari that I'm your favorite."

"She probably already knows."

"Yeah, but no need to rub it in her face."

We come to a stop at the end of the hallway. Emilio spins around to face me. "Wait here," he says, then disappears into the party room. Less than a minute later, he reappears with a gift bag in his hand.

"I'm not off for another two hours and I wanted to give you this ahead of time."

I'm kinda speechless. Gifts aren't his MO.

"Open it," he encourages.

I reach over and take the bag from him, then gently pull the stuffing out and peek inside. Resting at the bottom is a brand-new sketchbook and a case of sketching pencils. I suck in a sharp breath. My gaze immediately finds his.

"Emilio—"

He cuts me off.

"I know it's not your first sketchbook, but it's your first professional one. You're going to need it in design school because you're going to kill the competition."

Tears well in my eyes. "You're crazy."

"Hush. I don't want to hear it. Just say thank you and accept the gift."

I smile harder than I have in weeks, completely overcome with emotion. "Thank you so much. They'll both be put to good use."

"I know they will," he assures. He steps back and motions his head toward the party room. "Now get in there. You've got people waiting, but you didn't hear that from me."

Excitement floods my chest. I lean up on my tiptoes to kiss his cheek and stride past him. I sneak another glance inside the bag, antsy to draw up some new sketches. Holding off until school starts isn't an option anymore. Not when I have access to these.

I drop my clutch inside the bag and grab both handles, then push the doors wide open. Once I step inside, all my closest friends and family pop out from behind tables and surprise me. I give them my best oh-my-god-I-never-saw-this-coming face and hope they buy it.

Twinkling lights and flickering candles cast a magical glow over the room, radiating a sense of warmth. Being surrounded by unconditional love helps, too. Large platters of red velvet cupcakes grace the center of confetti-filled tables. Every last detail is well thought-out and perfectly executed, down to the design of the napkins. They're folded to look like black, strapless cocktail dresses with a ring of faux diamonds and pearls to hold it together around the waistline. My eyes scan the crowd for the one person who's responsible for managing every major and minor detail, not only for tonight's event, but for every milestone in my life—my mom. I spot her and mouth the words "thank you," even though it's not nearly enough.

Her smile bursts with pride as she mouths "love you" right back.

I take a moment to absorb everything. It's overwhelming, but in the best possible way. Mia and Tori both come running up, fully decked out in flapper headbands and long beads. I drop the gift bag and wrap an arm around each of them, going in for a group hug.

"Sorry for ditching you outside, but I had to get in here and warn everyone before you came in," Mia says into my ear.

I pull back to smile at her. "You're forgiven." My head twists in Tori's direction. "What are you doing here? I thought you were staying in San Marcos for the summer."

"Oh, bitch, please. Like I'd miss this party."

She twirls around to grab a headband and some beads off a nearby table, then she slips the pearls around my neck and carefully places the headband over my head.

"There," she says, satisfied. "Now you're sort of a flapper girl."

"Very 1920s of you," I praise.

"I did my homework."

"I'm impressed."

"All right you three, huddle together for a quick photo op," my mom interrupts.

We line up and wind our arms around each other's waists. Mom whips out her iPhone and counts to three. Seconds before she snaps the photo, Chase slips in through the doors and jumps in the shot for a glorious photobomb. Mia looks over her shoulder and pushes him backward.

"What?" he shrugs. "I'm extremely photogenic."

She grins and shakes her head, then focuses her attention on my mom for a retake. This time around, we get it right.

"Everyone grab a plate and feel free to help themselves," my mom announces. "Andre and I are going to run out front and get some pitchers so we have drinks."

"Sounds good," I say, grabbing a plate and stealing a cupcake. I peel the foil off the sides and lick the cream cheese frosting.

Mom's a goddess.

That's all there is to it.

I eat, then make my rounds, hitting up every person who took the time to come out and celebrate tonight. Everyone's curious what my long-term goals are and whether or not I plan on coming back to Austin. Not having the slightest idea of what lies ahead, I keep it very noncommittal. It's strange not to have everything mapped out. Liberating, but strange.

Later in the evening, as guests start trickling out the door, I use the brief window of opportunity to sneak off to a bathroom stall and check my phone for any missed calls or texts. I wrestle the device out of my clutch and stare down at the screen. A spasm assaults my chest.

MDJD: *Congratulations on your acceptance, Rave. I'm so fucking proud of you and how far you've come. Celebrate hard because you deserve it. Miss you like a drug, love you like a cure.*

Seeing his words displayed across my screen softens every part of me. I hate the affect he has on my heart. I hate that he's not here to make it better. I hate that every time I'm alone, my body aches for his touch. Love is supposed to make you strong, not weak. So why do I feel shortchanged? I gave it my all and he walked away. Maybe I'm the one who should've left. How do we know when to keep fighting and when to forfeit?

I'm tempted to type out a response, but I don't want to give him the wrong impression. What's done is done. There's no turning back. He made his choice and now we both have to live with it. Still, knowing he's out there thinking about me, wherever he is, gives me a small sliver of satisfaction.

Chalking it up to a momentary lapse in judgment, I hit reply.

Me: *I miss you too. I'm sorry for all the times we fought over stupid stuff. It seems so trivial now. I should've been more understanding when you needed me.*

MDJD: *Rave, I told you there was nothing you could've done. Let it go.*

Me: *I can't. I just feel like it's time for me to own up to my part. I know how judgmental I can be sometimes.*

MDJD: *I'm no walk in the park either. We both fucked up, and we're both learning from our mistakes. Now quit stealing my traits ;).*

That one makes me smile.

Me: *Please know that I hope you find what you're looking for.*

I put my phone on silent and drop it back in my clutch, vowing not to look at it for the rest of the night.

I don't even last fifteen minutes. Doesn't matter anyway because there's no response.

TWENTY

e r i c

I'm staring at a blank canvas when a sense of impending doom travels up my spine, causing every hair on the back of my neck stand straight up. I set down the paint can and walk over to the window and peer through the blinds. Just as I suspected, Mom's pulling into the driveway. I glance down at my phone. She's twenty-five minutes late. Could've sworn she was gonna flake. Secretly wish she would have. She's interrupting my painter's block and derailing my busy schedule. I had a full day planned of lying out in the sun, doing nothing. A much-needed sign that I need to get back to real life. Unemployment was fun while it lasted, but I'm beyond bored and broke.

What else is new?

Mom steps out of the car with a bag of chips in her hand. She dusts leftover crumbs off her jean shorts, then bends down to grab a beach bag and slings it over her shoulder. Does she think we're going swimming or something?

Holy shit. What if that's an overnight bag?

I'm royally screwed.

A gust of wind blows her blonde out of her face and ruffles her blouse. I can feel her stare at me, even though her eyes are hidden beneath a pair of thick black shades. She nods, then she pushes the car door shut and walks my way. I take a calming breath and brace myself, moving to the front door to let her in.

"Hey there," she greets, stepping inside. She lifts her sunglasses onto her head and takes a sweeping glance around the room.

I close the door behind her and ease back.

"Hey yourself. What's with the bag?"

Her gaze drops to the tote. "Oh, I brought some beach stuff in case this turns into an all-day thing."

Thank God. She's not staying the night. My body relaxes slightly.

"You seem…different," she notes, her eyes appraising me.

Interesting comment coming from someone who barely knows me.

"Want something to drink?" I offer.

"Yeah, an iced tea or a water would be great."

I disappear into the kitchen and grab a clean glass from the dishwasher. Opening the fridge, I pour a glass of tea, then set the pitcher back inside and steal a handful of ice from the freezer. Mom sets her tote, keys, and chips on the counter. She wanders over to the back door and stares out the window, soaking up the ocean view.

"It's so beautiful here."

"Have you been to Crystal Beach before?"

She shakes her head. "I've lived in Austin all my life and I've never been down here. Crazy, huh?"

I shrug even though she can't see it. "Not really. I think many people share a similar experience. When you live so close to a place like this, you don't appreciate it like you should. You either spend so much time here that you're desensitized, or you put it off thinking there's always going to be another tomorrow. But time gets away from you and excuses start piling up. Same recipe for everything else in life. Then, before you know it, you've been confined to what you're familiar with, and the wild dreams and exhilarating travel plans you once had fade away and become nothing more than *woulda coulda shouldas*. It's cruel and unusual punishment. Death by complacency."

No clue where that rant came from.

She glances over her shoulder, an array of different emotions dance across her face. "There are far worse things than mediocrity, Eric. Trust me. I've straddled that line for years. But you did just describe my entire life in one depressing paragraph."

I shut my mouth and make an effort to curb the negativity. Closing the space between us, I hand her the iced tea.

"Thanks," she says, looking down. She swirls the ice around in her glass, then takes a sip. "Just out of curiosity, does your uncle know I'm here?"

"Nope. He didn't even want me here, so I thought I'd leave that part out."

She nods, understanding.

"We used to be close, you know. Max and I—we were inseparable."

"What happened?"

Her eyes find mine. "You."

Here we go again. I'm always the scapegoat. The sole reason why her life never turned out quite the way it was supposed to. Big mistake asking that question. I look away and clench my jaw, trying my hardest to conceal how much that one hurt.

"I didn't mean it like that," she insists.

"You never do," I mutter bitterly.

She moves in front of me so we're standing face to face. "He didn't approve of me giving you up. That's what caused the rift. He tried to talk me out of it several times. Said I was making the wrong decision and I was more capable of raising a child than I was giving myself credit for. Deep down, I think he was scared of what would happen if he took you in. We both were."

I make eye contact and swallow, working up the courage to ask the one question I've been dying to ask for the last fourteen years. "Do you regret it?"

She ponders that for a few beats. "Yes and no. I relinquished custody because at that moment in time, I truly believed that's what was best for you. I couldn't provide any stability. I was yanking you around from place to place, making us both miserable. Financially, we were strapped. Raising a kid felt like an impossible task. I had youth and ignorance working against me, not to mention all the emotional baggage from my trauma. But make no mistake, giving you up was one of the hardest things I've ever had to do. If you were to ask me whether I'd do it all over again knowing what I know now, I'm not sure I would. Either way, I'm pleased with how you've turned out. It makes me proud."

An unexpected jolt of anger races through me. Who does this woman think she is? She doesn't get to be proud. She is not, nor will she ever be, a frontrunner in my success. And for her to insinuate otherwise is a bald-faced lie and an insult. She wasn't even around for half my childhood. And the half she was present for she was a passive participant, at best. Newsflash: bare minimum effort is what separates a donor from a true parent. As someone who's the former, she needs to stop overstepping her bounds and behaving like a parent who put in all the work.

"What's going on with you lately? Why are you acting like this?"

Her forehead creases. "What do you mean?"

"Why are you so chill and secure all of a sudden? For years you've resented me and gone out of your way to break me down, convincing me that I was somehow responsible for ruining your life. And now you show up here with a warm and fuzzy attitude, telling me you've had a change of heart, and that maybe I wasn't so bad after all. Surely you can understand my confusion?"

She sets her iced tea on the counter and motions her head towards the living room. I stay put, trying to figure out what her angle is.

"Come on, Eric."

Reluctantly, I follow. She takes a seat on the couch and pats the cushion next to her, inviting me to do the same. I waltz past her and opt for the ottoman instead. Too soon for family bonding. I plop down and stretch my legs out, crossing my feet at the ankles. We stare at each other, unblinking.

"Remember the last time you came to visit me?"

I nod, recalling the day I went there to tell her about Raven, and she was busy screwing some married guy.

"After you said those things and stormed out, I reached a breaking point. I realized that I was sick of being unhappy and carrying all that pain around. I started seeing a therapist, and she's been helping me deal with things I should've dealt with over twenty years ago." She averts her gaze and shifts around awkwardly.

I stiffen, preparing for what's coming next. Neither one of us wants to broach the forbidden subject, but it's long overdue. She deserves to be heard. And so do I.

I wait patiently while she formulates her thoughts.

Her eyes find mine again. The uncertainty that was there moments ago has been replaced with determination. "As you know, when I was a sophomore in high school, I was raped. It was one of the most terrifying experiences of my life. Everything I thought I knew about trust and safety had been violated. My happiness, my sense of security, my self-worth...all of it was gone." She pauses and swallows. "When you're forced to endure something like that, it takes you to a very dark, desolate place. I didn't tell anyone right away because I was afraid of what people might say. I was traumatized, and I didn't want to be judged on top of it. I knew all the kids at school would talk if given the chance, and I couldn't face the prospect of people finding out. So, I kept it quiet.

"For a long time I blamed myself, unable to forget that if I hadn't snuck out and gone to that party, it never would've happened. I imagined a thousand different scenarios where the outcome could've been different, but it just made everything that much harder to deal with. Harboring all that shame and turmoil arguably did just as much damage to me as the actual assault, but it felt like there was no one to turn to, no one to confide in. I channeled all my pain into hating him. It was the only way I could survive and feel in control.

"A few weeks later, I found out I was pregnant. Words can't even describe the level of terror I experienced when that test came back positive. I thought my life was over." Tears gradually begin to fall down her face. "I was too young to have a kid. I had no job, no money, no one to depend on, and no way out of this situation that someone else put me in without my consent. Eventually, I had no choice but to come clean and tell my parents. They immediately linked me up with a counselor, but it was too late. The damage had been done. Abortion seemed like the only viable option."

Those last seven words ring out loud and clear. I narrow my gaze and study her reaction. I don't want to know this about her. It's too painful. I don't want to know that someone violated her in the worst possible way and left her with no other options. She wasn't even old enough to smoke, vote, drink, or get a tattoo, but she was having a kid. A kid she never asked for and didn't want. Believe it or not, I can sympathize. But on the same token, nobody asked me what I wanted. I didn't choose to be born this way. And I never wanted to be someone else's burden. She needs to realize that I was a victim, too. Before I can jump in and tell her that, she picks up where she left off.

"I'd been saving up all my babysitting money and borrowing cash from friends to afford the procedure. Once I called the clinic and found out how much it would cost, they told me I needed parental consent because I was underage. I begged my parents to sign off, but they refused. That felt like the ultimate betrayal. The two people who I had idolized and depended on the most in this world had sealed my fate and left me to face this all alone. I hated them for it. We got into an explosive argument. I told them it was my body, my choice, and if they wouldn't respect that, I was moving out. I ended up packing my bags and leaving the very same night."

"Have you talked to them since?" I ask.

"On occasion."

"I owe them my life, you know," I say, my tone sharp and accusatory. "They spoke up for me when I didn't have a voice, which is more than you've ever done for me."

She winces, but I don't stop there.

"Do you have any idea what it feels like to be your son? To know that my own mother never wanted me and would've done anything to get rid of me?" My throat clogs up with emotion. "For twenty-six years I've carried that feeling around inside. You think I'm your burden? Think again. You're my burden." The second those spiteful words leave my mouth guilt consumes me.

She stares at me with a look of resignation, like she's forced to accept that this is what we've become. Back in the day, I would've reveled in this reaction. The more hurtful, the better. But now that she's sitting in front of me, desperately trying to connect, the only thing that registers is shame. It's much harder to despise my mom when her pain is so visceral and real. The whole experience is humanizing. Bottom line: we're all products of our parents' unresolved issues. It's unavoidable. But I don't want to live like this anymore. I also don't want the cycle to continue on with my own kids. It has to stop somewhere, so why not with me?

My shoulders sink with defeat.

"I'm sorry for what happened to you, Mom. Sincerely, I am. But that's not my fault. Quit trying to make me take ownership. That's *his* fault. No one else's. You didn't deserve what happened to you and neither did I, but it happened to us anyway. Now we have to figure out a way to move forward. We were victims and now we're survivors and next we'll be goddamn champions because we're going to pull through this nightmare in one severely cracked piece. And if you're not willing to get on board with that and seek out a better life, then I'm cutting ties. The choice is yours."

Her gaze drops to the floor. Suddenly, everything feels very raw and exposed. I don't shy away from it, though. Progress.

"Did you ever think twice about going through with it?" I ask after a few beats.

"Of course I did. Making a decision to terminate a pregnancy is never simple or easy, especially when you're the one going through it. The constant back and forth weighs on your soul. At least, for me it did. But bringing you into this world and raising you under all those circumstances didn't feel right either."

She leans forward and clasps her hands, her face becoming serious.

"I need you to understand something, Eric. Despite everything I've confessed, you are, and always will be, the best thing to come out of that situation. I love you infinitely. That feeling has stayed with me since your first breath, and it'll be there long after your last. Maybe I didn't want you in the beginning, but when I finally had you, my heart inflated with so much love it hurt. I didn't want to be responsible for screwing you up. I told myself I'd rather have the heartache of losing you to Max than the guilt of failing you. I'm sorry things didn't work out that way. But before you decide to crucify me, please keep in mind that I was a traumatized kid who was scared to death of the unknown and had no clue how to handle it."

I exhale and run my hands through my hair, glancing up at the ceiling and allowing the tears to flow. "Jesus. We're so fucked up, Mom."

"But we're fighters," she retorts. "And we'll figure this out together."

I lower my chin. "How?"

"We'll start with therapy."

"And after?"

"Then we'll get to know each other again…if you're open to it," she adds, not wanting to push anything on me prematurely.

We have such a long way to go, but it's a start. Repairing the relationship won't be easy, but hopefully it'll be worth it. I have to trust my gut and go with it. The upside is it can't get much worse. If the idea of cutting ties with her seems better than our current situation, then we're about as shattered as we can possibly be.

I nod my acceptance.

She slumps back against the couch, her actions mirroring how I feel inside: exhausted, relieved, and cautiously optimistic. For the next several minutes we sit in silence, reflecting on everything that's happened. I glance over at the counter. Her glass of tea is covered in beads of sweat, the ice mostly melted.

Her soft voice cuts in. "What have you been painting recently?"

My gaze drifts to the blank canvas that's been sitting there for days.

"Absolutely nothing," I answer, bringing my attention back to her. "Can't seem to get inspired these days."

"Why not?"

"It's complicated."

"So un-complicate it."

I don't want to delve that deep. We're not ready. The less she knows about Raven, the better. When you find your person, you try your damnedest to shield them from any baggage that comes along with you. I may not have always been successful, but it wasn't for lack of effort. Like it or not, Mom's still baggage. And even though Rave and I aren't together anymore, I'm still protective of her.

"What's her name?" my mom asks, sensing my struggle.

"I'd rather not discuss it."

"Is it the girl you wanted to tell me about a few months ago?"

I keep my lips sealed and my expression unreadable, refusing to budge on this one. She drops the subject and tries for a different one.

"What about painting?"

"What about it?"

"Are you in the mood?"

"Mom, I already told you it's not happening."

"Oh, come on. Meet me halfway."

I clench my jaw to stifle my irritation. For years I've adopted the mentality that this woman doesn't deserve shit from me. Retraining myself not to think that way takes constant reinforcement, and a lot of getting used to.

"Fine. We'll paint. But I'm telling you right now, the only one who will be painting anything worthwhile is you."

I stand up and gather all the supplies. The tarp is already laid out from my last failed attempt. And the one before that. I toss her a can and move back, allowing her to step into my universe. She shakes the can vigorously and spouts the first streak of paint. Watching her reminds me of being a kid again. The way she fearlessly attacks the canvas, pouring all of her emotion into layers of vibrant color. My eyes close as I breathe in the fumes. I've never considered art to be my calling, but honestly, I can't imagine doing anything else. Nothing compares. One of the many things I've discovered about myself since being here.

Somewhere in the middle, my mom decides to stop and offers me the can. I shake my head. She sticks her hand out farther, prompting me. Reluctantly, I seize it and step forward to finish what she started. I visualize Raven's face to try and conjure up some inspiration. Then, I proceed to do something I haven't done in months; I paint. All it takes is a few lines for the creative barrier to collapse. Every repressed emotion comes flooding out and releases onto the canvas, freeing me. And if that experience wasn't notable enough, something even more remarkable happened:

Today, I met my mother.

TWENTY-ONE

e r i c

After finishing up my Skype session with Dr. Coleman, I pack up my bags and venture outside. Beaches are overrated. I'm ready to get the hell out of here. A heavy dose of perma-vacation boredom was all it took for me to realize I'm not built for this shit. Didn't help that Mom overstayed her welcome and ended up bouncing a few days ago. She and I are supposed to start family therapy next month. We'll see how that one goes. Not holding my breath in case she decides to revert back to being a vapid narcissist.

Stay positive, Eric.

Hope for the best; prepare for the worst.

To give her props, she appears to have a firm grasp on reality. No more of this noncommittal, I-refuse-to-take-ownership-of-my-transgressions bullshit. Only took twenty-six years to reach that point, but alas, we've arrived. Forecast for family bonding looks promising. Chances of selective perception have decreased; meanwhile, compromise is gaining momentum.

I throw my bag into the truck, climb inside, and start her up. A memory flashes before my eyes when I stare at the window in front of me. A little boy standing alone, watching the driveway, tears streaming down his face. An echo of gravel crunching beneath the tires reverberates in his ears. Abandonment finds a new soul to burrow in.

I was that kid.

Only this time, nobody's getting ditched.

Grinning, I throw the truck in reverse and crank up the music. "It's My Life" by The Animals blasts through the speakers. I lower the windows, throw one arm up on the steering wheel, and belt out the lyrics.

My paint-splotched fingers drum along to the beat. Head bobs to and fro. Raven's Audrey Hepburn pendant sways from side to side, secured from the mirror above. A gust of fresh air causes my shirt to flutter against my skin. I glance in the rearview mirror and chuck up the deuces to a rapidly shrinking Crystal Beach.

Four-and-a-half hours later, I swerve into Raven's apartment complex with an empty stomach, a full bladder, less than a quarter tank of gas, 12% battery life on my phone, and 2% worth of patience left. The clock on my dash reads 3:12 p.m., which actually means it's 4:12. Should've stopped home to shower beforehand, but I'm too anxious and excited to see her. Totally unable to decipher which one is more prominent. My heart hasn't been this strung out since my heroin days.

Kidding, only kidding.

I jump out of the truck and take a sweeping glance around the parking lot. No sign of Raven's car. My feet carry me to the stairs and tackle them two at a time until I reach her door.

Knock, knock, knock.

I do the potty dance for a hot minute, then knock again—more forcefully this time.

No answer.

She's probably at work or with Mia. I huff an exasperated breath and sprint back down to my truck, praying to God I don't piss myself along the way. I cruise out of the parking lot, debating whether to call Mia. I don't want to deplete my battery life even more. The girl likes to talk, and I'm not in a particularly chatty mood—unless Raven's there.

Thinking, thinking….

Nope. Not worth the risk. Our convo needs to be done in person.

Remembering that Mia lives with Chase now, I hop on Mopac and head in that direction. Fifteen minutes and an aching bladder later, I burst through their door without knocking and race to the nearest bathroom like I'm experiencing a severe case of the Taco Bell shits.

Instant relief follows.

Toilet flushes.

Hands get washed.

Footsteps register at the exact moment the door flies open to reveal a bold yet confused Chase. He observes the scene.

"Dude, what the *fuck*?"

Outstanding formal introduction.

"I had to go, man," I stress. "You don't even understand. I almost gave myself a golden shower on the way over."

Mia's voice cuts in.

"Eric?"

I lean past the doorframe and give her a sexy smirk.

"Oh, my God!" she runs up and collides with me. My arms instinctively wrap around her torso and lift her up off the ground. "Hey, Strawberry."

She wiggles free, unable to contain her excitement, and smacks the side of my arm. "Where the hell have you been? We missed you."

"Sorry. Needed to get away and recharge."

"Took you long enough. Next time keep us in the loop," she warns. "You've chewed me out for using the exact same tactic, remember?"

Girl's got a point.

I sneak past them and head for the kitchen. "I know, I know. I'm an asshole. I should've called."

"When did you get back into town?" Chase inquires, trailing two steps behind me.

"Like, twenty minutes ago. I stopped by Raven's place, but she must be at work or something." I come to a gradual halt and spin around to face them. "Figured she was with you two. Obviously not."

Chase and Mia both tense up and exchange a knowing look.

"What?" I ask, eyes darting between them.

Mia's expression becomes apologetic.

"Raven's gone."

I blink a few times, not fully processing what she said. It takes a moment or two, but then it hits me like a ton of bricks. My throat goes dry.

"What? Where?"

"She left for Cali about a week ago," Chase answers.

My chest tightens. She left without saying goodbye? Dead silence falls over the room. Feels like someone just pulled the rug out from under me. Here I was under the impression I had some extra time set aside to prepare myself and make amends. She's long gone, and everyone knew it but me.

My fists ball up. I shoot Chase an accusatory glare. "You told me I had a month left. That was three weeks ago. What the hell happened?"

"She bumped up the date," Mia explains.

"And y'all didn't think to update me?"

"It was a snap decision. We barely got any notice ourselves," Chase responds.

Mia nods in agreement. "He's right. She stopped by the morning of to say goodbye, then she left. You never would've made it back in time."

Caught in a daze, I sink back against the wall for support. My legs feel weak, and my heart feels heavy. The combination drags me straight to the floor. How did this happen? Things weren't supposed to turn out this way. I was going to come back and surprise her. Tell her everything I should've said a long time ago. Indulge her about my past. Fantasize about the future—our future. Profess my undying love for her. Now it's too late.

Mia crouches down in front of me and makes eye contact. She doesn't have to say anything. The look on her face says it all.

"I'm so sorry, Eric."

I nod absently, unable to form a single thought.

She tilts her head up toward Chase. He shrugs in response, not knowing what to say. Her worried gaze swings back to mine. "Is there anything I can do?"

Just as I'm about to shake my head no, an idea strikes. I slap my palms against the wood floor animatedly. Mia reels back in surprise. I hop to my feet, and she automatically follows suit.

"What do you need?" she asks.

"Give me her address."

TWENTY-TWO

r a v e n

For the last couple weeks, I've been settling into my new life and getting acclimated to my surroundings. It hasn't been without its challenges. An hour ago, I was on the verge of tears. As of now, I'm in love. It switches constantly. Classes don't start for another six weeks, but I wanted to come out here early to establish myself and make the transition as smooth as possible. Aside from the panic attacks—every hour on the hour—it's going swimmingly.

Living conditions are a joke. I'm in a crappy, rundown studio apartment because it's the only thing I can afford out here. The place is half-furnished and seriously under-decorated. My body is surviving solely on microwavable Spanish rice, mac 'n' cheese, and boxed wine. I try not to complain, though. This was my decision. Pursuing my dream is worth the sacrifice. Must keep reminding myself that there are people out there in the world with real problems who would kill for my situation.

Perspective—it's jarring.

On the upside, I've made a new friend. Her name is Everly. She lives down the street in an even crappier studio apartment and is quite literally a starving musician. I've concluded that this is how all the skinny bitches stay slim—food deprivation. And not necessarily by their own accord. Although, there are plenty of *those* types walking around, too. Guess I can kiss my curves goodbye for the time being. Until I can afford to eat real food, I'm stuck on the welfare diet.

The biggest challenge I'm facing is being jobless. Traffic here rivals Austin's, so Metro is the new limo. Good thing I found a place near the University that's within walking distance. Mission *Land A J.O.B.* has commenced. Prospects are slightly disheartening, but the high turnover rates aren't. I'm biding my time for a phone call. Fingers crossed.

I take a short break from sketching designs and glance around at the beautiful scenery. I'm sitting on a park bench in Arlington Garden, enjoying a macchiato and soaking up the warm rays. Being outside helps me combat homesickness. I don't know why, but whenever I'm outdoors, my future seems brighter, my dreams so much more attainable. In a city where the possibilities are endless and the rejection is vast, all or nothing stakes force you to really live. Also, I like the people watching. Everything goes, fashion-wise in Southern Cali. So many unique ideas.

Suddenly, the sound of a child's laughter steals my attention. I twist my head and stare over my shoulder. An adorable little girl, probably no older than four or five, is busy playing in the wildflowers. I smile reflexively. As if she can sense me watching, she glances up and freezes. When she decides that I'm not Stranger Danger, she comes trotting over, her tight ringlets bouncing with every step.

"Hi!" she exclaims in her miniature voice.

She tucks her arms behind her back and sways from side to side like she's proud of herself for making the first move. *Bolder and braver than many men I've encountered.* I set my coffee down on the bench and unfold my legs, then lean forward just a tad—enough to be friendly, but not intimidating.

"Hello there. What's your name?"

"I'm Lily. *Not* after the flower."

"That's a very pretty name," I praise. "My name is Raven. *Not* after the bird."

She smiles at our mutual connection.

"How old are you, Lily?"

"Four." She gets on her tippy toes, her curious little eyes peering over the top of my sketchbook. "Whatcha drawing?"

"Dresses."

"I like dresses."

"Do you?" I tilt the sketchbook toward her so she can see clearly. "What do you think of these?"

She rocks back on her heels and ponders. "Hmmm. They're pretty, but they need color."

"Oh, don't worry. They will. These are just the outlines." I explain.

"Okay, good," she says, relief evident in her small features. "Having no color is soooo boring."

Couldn't agree more. Is it possible I have a little fashionista on my hands? Someone call up Anna Wintour and tell her I found a prodigy. This one doesn't pull any punches. It's that unfiltered quality children possess. They say what they mean and mean what they say. At least when it's coming from a four-year-old, it's cute and endearing. Perhaps I'll get lucky and all my professors will be repressed children trapped inside adult-sized bodies.

Doubtful. Very doubtful.

Her lips drop open. "You should make a princess gown!"

"You think so?"

She nods emphatically.

I chuckle at her enthusiasm. "Maybe I will."

"Lily!" a voice hollers.

Her eyes widen. "Uh-oh. That's my mom. I gotta go."

"Okay. Bye."

She starts to run off but circles back around. "When you make that princess gown, make sure you give her a sword, too."

"I like how you think. You already know how to accessorize."

She grins, waves adiós, and dashes off.

We're all so eager to grow up and become adults, and then we get here and realize it's not all that it's cracked up to be. Things that were once so beautifully effortless become overly complex. Love, friendship, forgiveness, dreams—all so much easier to navigate during childhood. Every crucial decision was made by playing eeny, meeny, miny, moe, and potential love interests were left to the fate of flower petals.

He loves me. He loves me not.

Speaking of love interests....

Nope. Not going there. Too painful. It was so much easier to keep everything contained when I was surrounded by friends and family. Being deprived of his love is tormenting. It's almost as bad as receiving it. Because once you experience something so powerful, so all-consuming, you can never really go back to the way you were before. And anything that comes after pales in comparison.

*Annnd...*there goes the urge to sketch.

Feeling tapped out, I close my sketchbook, grab my coffee, and traipse to the nearest Metro station.

Forty minutes later, I arrive back at the complex. I slip inside the door and gingerly climb the stairs, fishing my key out of my front pocket. Can't wait to crawl into my bed and crash. When I reach the hallway, my feet come to an abrupt halt.

What the...?

My heart begins pounding furiously. Breathing becomes shallow.

Eric's sitting outside my door, browsing on his phone, unaware that I'm watching.

What is he doing here? I close my eyes and reopen them to make sure my mind isn't playing tricks on me.

Negative.

I stay put, unsure of what to do. Half of me wants to sneak back out while I still have the chance, and the other half wants to sprint in his direction. Am I supposed to let him in? It's not like I can kick him out. He traveled all the way here. But why?

I tilt my head toward the ceiling and curse my love life—or lack thereof. I straighten my shoulders and start walking toward him. When he hears me approaching, he glances up with a hopeful expression on his face. It's a look that squeezes my heart. He hops to his feet and slides his phone into his pocket, prepared to give me his full attention.

I come to a smooth stop in front of him and stare. He waits patiently for me to say something. I've got nothing. I still can't even wrap my brain around the fact that he's here. The corners of his mouth lift into a grin. Something's different about him. There's a sense of ease that wasn't there before. He looks happy. Peaceful. And utterly handsome, but that's nothing new.

He clears his throat to break the ice. "I, uh...hope you don't mind that I waited here."

I do.

But not really.

"How long have you been waiting?"

He glances down to check the time on his phone. "About an hour."

"Wanna come in?"

I can tell he wants to say something sarcastic, but refrains. "Yeah, that'd be cool."

I shove my empty coffee container in his hand and step in front to unlock the door. He inches closer, making me hyperaware of his presence. My fingers fumble with the key like some blind drunk chick. When I finally manage to get the door open, he follows me inside, kicks it shut, and surveys the apartment.

"A studio, huh? This must be killing you."

"It's not that bad," I lie.

He gives me an amused look, knowing better. "You're on my level now."

I ignore him and flip on the kitchen light. It flickers a few times, then casts a dull glow over the room. The incessant buzzing noise is an added bonus. I set my sketchbook and keys down, then rest my back against the edge of the counter.

"Where's the trash?" he asks.

I point below the sink. He walks over and discards my cup, then stands in front of me, invading my personal space. My body's natural inclination is to curl into him, so I do the opposite and lean back with nowhere to go. Having him here feels so normal, yet so strange. It's as if no time has passed, even though it's been almost six weeks. That's half a season. But who's counting?

He swallows. "How have you been?"

"Depends on the day. I'm dealing in my own way. I'm sure you can relate."

He nods. "You have no idea how much I've missed you."

I choose to bypass that comment entirely. "You seem different."

He rubs the back of his neck like he always does when he's feeling uncomfortable or vulnerable. "Yeah. A lot has happened since I last saw you."

"Anything you care to share?"

For a brief moment our eyes lock and it's as if he can hear the onslaught of questions running rampant through my mind.

He exhales a heavy breath. "A lot, actually."

He wanders into the living room, which also happens to be my bedroom. He plants his hands on his hips and stares out the window, deep in thought. I have an overwhelming urge to walk up behind him and wrap my arms around his torso for comfort, but I can't seem to move.

"I'm slowly working on rebuilding a relationship with my mom. She came to visit me at my uncle's beach house and we were able to talk through some things. We have a long way to go, but we're in family therapy and learning how to move forward."

"That's great, Eric." I wasn't expecting that.

"We laid everything out on the table. Good and bad. She's actually doing pretty well." He makes eye contact. "I have faith in her, Rave. It's different this time. We've covered more ground in one month than we have in my entire life."

Hearing him call me "Rave" makes my stomach flutter like I'm fourteen again. Plenty of my friends use that nickname, but whenever Eric says it, it's so much more intimate and personal. It's not just a term of endearment; it's a branding.

"I'm so glad y'all are on the same page. I've wanted you to be happy for so long and seeing you this way makes everything worth it. I feel like you're finally getting everything you wanted. Happiness, peace, and stability."

"Yep. There's only one thing missing."

He saunters over and places his hands on the countertop, caging me in. I couldn't even tell you how fast my heart is beating because I have no idea what the hell happened to it. Logic tells me to push him away and be done with it. My heart wants to pull him closer and kiss him senseless.

He rests his forehead against mine and closes his eyes. "I want my girl back."

My shoulders go lax. A glimpse of a silver linked chain around his neck catches my attention. It looks oddly familiar. The tips of my fingers brush along the side of his neck as I pull the chain out from underneath his collar. He drops his gaze to the Audrey Hepburn pendant displayed in my palm.

"Thought I'd return it."

"I didn't even know you had this. It went missing a couple months ago."

"That's because I swiped it before I left. I wanted a little piece of you after the breakup, so I stuffed it in my duffel bag ahead of time. Sorry I didn't mention anything."

I release the pendant. "I'm not going back to Austin."

The corners of his mouth lift into a smirk. "How convenient. Neither am I."

"What are you talking about?"

"Got a job at an art gallery nearby."

Poof!

Romantic haze dissipates.

"Oh, my God. You got a job? Are you freaking kidding me?!" I've been applying nonstop and he secured a job before he even crossed the California border? Lies.

He steps back, confused by my outburst. "Why are you so upset? I meant it when I said I was coming back for you."

"Yeah, and I meant it when I said don't bother." I duck under his arm and put some much-needed space between us. No way am I going to let him charm me out of my common sense. I grind my teeth together, debating where to begin.

"You are the most impulsive, exasperating son-of-a-bitch I've ever met. Certifiably crazy and unforgivably stubborn. You had no business coming out here and putting me in this position, assuming I'd be okay with it. And now you've given me no choice. Do you think that's fair? I'm out here trying to make it on my own, and all of a sudden you barge in without any warning and expect me to forgive and forget. You still haven't apologized for all the heartache you put me through last time. *Or* the time before that."

"Relax," he says calmly, walking towards me. "I wasn't banking on you agreeing to this, and I wasn't trying to derail any of your dreams or hard work. I'm out here to pursue art. Yes, obviously you're a major reason why I chose this location, but as per usual, it isn't all about you."

"Don't even—"

He presses his index finger against my lips. "Shut up and let me finish."

I narrow my gaze and reconsider kicking him out. He cups my face and tilts it upward, his eyes burning with emotion.

"You should know that I reached this decision after I took a step back from you—from us. I had to dismantle our relationship in order to find my identity. You've had yours figured out from the very beginning, but for me, it wasn't so simple. I was lost. But I'm not anymore and you're partially to blame. Being around you, seeing how fearless you are when it comes to your dreams, it's made me more ambitious. I've always admired you, even when we were in high school. But then I fell in love with you, and everything else became a thousand times more inspiring. You're my muse, Rave. Not just in art, but in life."

That is by far the greatest compliment I've ever received.

Ugh, it's so hard to stay mad at him when he opens up.

"So here's the plan; I'm going to hunt for a place of my own, and when I get settled in, I'm going to start taking you out on dates and apologizing profusely until you learn to like me again. Third time's a charm." He pauses. "Or in our case, maybe the fourth." He shakes his head and refocuses. "Whatever. We're bound to get it right eventually."

"And what if we break up?" I ask.

"What if I just marry you instead?"

Hope blooms in my chest. *Not so fast.* "Be serious."

"I am. This is it for me. I know it'll take a while to prove that to you, but I'll spend as much time as it takes earning your trust back.

I love you. And it's time I started treating you that way. I never wanted to hurt you, but I was convinced I had to do everything on my own. I learned not to depend on anyone because almost every person in my life was unreliable. But you never should've been grouped into that category. For that, I'm sorry."

"Where are you going to stay in the meantime?"

"I was planning on sleeping in the truck."

"You drove out here?"

He nods. "Had to have at least *one* duck in the row. Besides, I wanted to bring my stuff. The rest of it is chillin' at my mom's place until further notice."

"You know I'm not going to let you sleep in the truck, right? Not after you drove all the way out here."

"I was secretly hoping you'd say that."

"You can take the floor and I'll take the futon. Once I like you again, I'll consider sharing the bed."

"Give me twenty-four hours," he says with a gleam in his eye.

"Don't push it."

He smiles and leans forward to press his lips into mine.

I jerk back. "What did I just say?"

"I already have heaps of bullshit to make up for anyway. Might as well put this one on my tab and make it worth the extra floor time."

Before I can protest, he kisses me. I inhale sharply. My eyes flutter closed and my hands slide around the back of his neck, pulling him closer, deepening the kiss. He breaks it and stares down at me, grinning like he just got everything he ever wanted. I grab the chain around his neck and yank him back to me. His hands grip my waist as he hoists me up onto the kitchen counter. He nudges himself between my legs and resumes kissing. We're all frantic hands and hungry mouths, heated breaths and blissful sighs. With every searing touch, he fills me back up, reviving me. Our clothes disintegrate. My back meets the floor with a thud. Eric hovers, his chest rising and falling as rapidly as my heart's beating.

"Totally worth the ire," he concludes.

His plants my hands on either side of my head and interlaces our fingers. My legs reflexively wrap around his torso. I stare longingly into his arctic eyes. The natural light pouring in from the windows intensifies the color. I want those eyes fixated on me forever. Without warning, he rocks his hips forward and takes me. My back arches in response. His moves are forceful, dominant. My skin burns against the rough carpet, the sensations rippling throughout my body.

I love him, I love him, I love him, is all I can think with each powerful thrust.

As if he can read my thoughts, he kisses me hard and passionate. His mouth swallows up my euphoric cries. Once I peak, he follows me there in a series of shudders.

Then we collapse.

We lay together in a sticky, sweaty mess, waiting for our hearts to stop racing and our breathing to slow. His cheek is pressed against my chest, my fingertips lightly tracing the contours of his back. He moans in appreciation.

"Surely you like me after that?" he mutters.

I laugh and use my weight to roll him off me and lay back. He leans up on an elbow and stares down at me with appreciation. He drops a kiss on my shoulder and brushes a stray hair out of my face.

"For the record, I wasn't kidding about marrying you. When you're done with design school, I'm pulling the trigger."

"Calm down. You haven't even gained access to the futon yet."

"Twenty-three hours and forty-six minutes to go."

I twist my head. "You're that convinced, huh?"

"You're *not?*"

Truth is, I am.

But just for fun, I'm going to make him suffer.

EPILOGUE

e r i c

I can't take my eyes off of my girl. Every time she sleeps, I pinch myself because it still doesn't feel real that we're back together. I've missed waking up to her every single morning. Making her breakfast, telling her how much I love her, how beautiful she is. Those things never get old. I've finally gained access to the bed, which means she likes me again. Sort of. I'm sure I'll be kicked to the floor again in no time. All the more reason to hurry up and get a different place. As much as I enjoy living here with Rave, it's too cramped and the floor is wreaking havoc on my back. She may not know it yet, but she's coming with me. We're upgrading to a one-bedroom apartment, even if it means I must work two jobs to swing the rent.

As each day passes, another piece of our trust restores. I can tell she half-expects me to dip out, but I'm not going anywhere. Not this time. I'm more than capable of opening up and being what she needs from here on out. Soon she'll realize that. And now that she's technically slumming it, she needs my help more than ever.

Dr. Coleman and I set up a Skype session so he can get caught up on everything that's happened. Unfortunately, because my mother lives in Texas, family therapy has been put on hold. To make up for that, she and I have been keeping in touch. She wants to fly out and meet Raven. I'm slowly warming up to the idea. Raven's all for it, but we'll see. Might as well get it over with, I guess. Introducing them sooner rather than later means we can all move forward. Barring any catastrophes, they'll be in-laws.

I know I said I'd wait until she's done with design school before popping the question, but I lied. It'll be in six months when we go home for Christmas. I've already found the ring and started planning. Six months may seem premature, but what can I say? If there's one person who I want to spend the rest of my life chasing, it's her. She deserves an epic love story, and I'm going to give her fleeting glimpses of one. It'll be *just* within her reach.

Out of the corner of my eye, I notice her stirring beneath the covers. A heavy yawn escapes her lips. I quietly wander over and sit down on the edge of the bed. The mattress dips beneath my weight, disturbing her. Sleepy brown eyes pop open.

"Morning," I greet, using my free hand to run my fingers through her hair.

She blinks a few times, then rolls onto her back and stretches, providing a spectacular view of her curves.

"Is that coffee in your hand?" she asks.

"Absolutely not."

"Liar. Hand it over."

"Get your own," I feign offense.

"How hot is it?"

"Scorching. Like our sex last night."

It was downright filthy. The things this girl can do to me, there's no equivalent. She rules my heart, and my body.

Her muscles relax into the sheets and her eyes glaze over with a dreamy haze.

I take a sip of coffee. "You're thinking about it, aren't you?"

"Nope. Thinking about that cup of coffee."

I lower the mug from my face and scowl.

Do you see what I have to put up with?

She props herself up on her forearms, clearly in a mood to negotiate. "Give me a few sips of that coffee, and I'll let you crawl back into this bed and do whatever you want."

Oh, hell yes. She can have the entire pot. All of it. With an attitude like that, I'll fly to Colombia and buy her some of the world's finest.

Undying love: it often comes in the form of caffeine.

With a steady hand, I pass off the mug. She steals it and takes a few sips.

"Drink faster," I order.

She closes her eyes, savoring the taste. Pretty sure she's doing that on purpose. She'll pay for that later. When they reopen, she gives me a sleepy-eyed, tousle-haired, sexy-but-insanely-cute smile. It's my favorite look, favorite feature, favorite everything. Cue another mental snapshot.

"That's enough coffee." I pry the mug from her fingers and set it down on the floor.

"Hey! I wasn't finished," she protests.

"Yes, you are."

I crawl onto the bed, grab her upper arms, and roll us over so she's on top.

She stares down at me with naughty eyes. "Tell me you love me," she demands.

"No way."

She leans down to kiss my neck. Her hot breath tickles my skin, causing my entire body to erupt in chills. She travels further up the side, nipping my earlobe. Soft palms caress my chest.

"Say it," she exhales into my ear.

"You say it first."

She brings her face close to mine so we're nose to nose. She bites her lip to stifle a grin. The energy is contagious. Like the sucker I am, I succumb and give her exactly what she wants. I can only deny the woman for so long.

"I love you."

I'm rewarded with another knockout smile. "Love you too, baby."

If I'm lucky enough, I'll have the privilege of hearing those words every day until we bite the dust. There'll be a few other choice words thrown in there, too, I'm sure. But then again, I suppose she's worth the hassle.

ACKNOWLEDGMENTS

A big thank you to Lisa Cerasoli, who was the very first person to see my potential and pipe up. You arguably put just as much hard work into this novel as I did. Thank you for pushing me (and boy did you push me on this one). It never ceases to amaze me how far you go for your clients. Two books down, countless more to go! As always, love you long time.

Thank you to Danielle Canfield for your hard work on the interior. I'm so pleased with how it turned out.

To Sarah Hansen at Okay Creations for a breathtaking cover. I told you exactly what I wanted, and you captured it brilliantly. So excited to work with you again on future projects.

To Anthony Fenner, your street art and lifestyle loosely inspired Eric.

To all the bloggers who read and reviewed this book, I can't thank you enough. You ladies are the backbone to an author's career. Real talk.

To my proofreaders, Carol Blodgett, Sandy Knott, Jamie Melton, Vicky Stafford, Cassie Findley, Rikki Schechinger, and Heather Brown: You girls rock. Thank you for all the time and effort you've spent critiquing my novel and giving me feedback.

To my parents, John Smith and Carole Lund-Smith, for supporting me along this journey and always encouraging me to pursue what I love.

To my brother, Zach Smith, for always encouraging me to take risks and challenge myself. I know you're patiently waiting for a non-romance book. It's coming, I promise.

To my husband, Ben Pratt, who deals with my shit on a daily basis. You are my rock. Thanks for putting up with the endless roller coaster of emotions, and for always believing in me, even when I don't always believe in myself. Olive juice.

And last but certainly not least, thank you to all the readers who've read, reviewed, and asked for more of my books. The feeling is indescribable. You are the reason I love what I do.

ABOUT THE AUTHOR

Lauren Michelle, who also writes under the name L.M. Pratt, is an editor by day and a writer by night. She's published three other novels—*Chasing Mia*, *Solstice*, and *Purgatory*. Lauren currently lives in Iowa with her husband Ben, her son Xander, and a golden retriever named Milo.

Connect with Lauren on Facebook and Instagram

Facebook: Author Lauren Michelle

Instagram: Lauren Michelle Pratt

catching
RAVEN